"Look At Me."

Stung, Barbara whirled and found herself confronting a hard-faced stranger.

"Thack, please!" The protest came from Ellie.

"I won't hurt her, Ellie. But I think it might be time for Miss Holcomb to grow up and face a few facts of life."

"I am fully aware of the facts of life, Mr. Sharp!" Almost instinctively, her hand hefted a detergent bottle.

"You lob that thing at me and you're in big trouble, honey."

Startled, Barbara looked at the bottle in her hand. She had never resorted to force before—never!

"Would you have tossed it?" A chuckle echoed from deep in Thack's throat.

"I—I don't know. But I was tempted."

"I'd have retaliated, you know." Barbara could feel Thack's warm breath caress her cheeks.

"You'd have, ah, thrown it back?"

"I was thinking more along the lines of throwing *you* back." His voice reflected his sexy smile. "Onto the floor—and under me."

Dear Reader,

Welcome to Silhouette! Our goal is to give you hours of unbeatable reading pleasure, and we hope you'll enjoy each month's six new Silhouette Desires. These sensual, provocative love stories are both believable and compelling—sometimes they're poignant, sometimes humorous, but always enjoyable.

Indulge yourself. Experience all the passion and excitement of falling in love along with our heroine as she meets the irresistible man of her dreams and together they overcome all obstacles in the path to a happy ending.

If this is your first Desire, I hope it'll be the first of many. If you're already a Silhouette Desire reader, thanks for your support! Look for some of your favorite authors in the coming months: Stephanie James, Diana Palmer, Dixie Browning, Ann Major and Doreen Owens Malek, to name just a few.

Happy reading!

Isabel Swift
Senior Editor

SDRL-7/85

JOAN HOHL
Texas Gold

Silhouette Desire

Published by Silhouette Books New York

America's Publisher of Contemporary Romance

SILHOUETTE BOOKS
300 East 42nd St., New York, N.Y. 10017

Copyright © 1986 by Joan Hohl

ISBN: 0-373-05294-4

First Silhouette Books printing July 1986

America's Publisher of Contemporary Romance

Printed in the U.S.A.

JOAN HOHL,

a Gemini and an inveterate daydreamer, says she always has her head in the clouds. Though she reads eight or nine books a week, she discovered romances only ten years ago. "But as soon as I read one," she confesses, "I was hooked." An extremely popular author, she is thrilled to be getting paid for exactly what she loves doing best.

Texas Gold is the first book of Joan's Trilogy for Desire. Right now, she is hard at work on the second book in the Metal Trilogy. If you liked Thack, you'll love Zack, his brother and the hero of *California Copper.* It will be a Silhouette Desire and should be coming out in the Fall of 1986.

For Elly—Nora Roberts
Pure gold all the way through.

One

The West Texas sun was merciless. Even with the air conditioner humming at full capacity, the small car was stifling. Her entire body misted with perspiration, Barbara Holcomb drew gulping breaths of stale air into her lungs and fought the urge to close her eyes against the brassy glare of sunlight.

Heat rays radiated from the road in front of her, creating an unreal, miragelike effect that strained her vision. The dry, fitful wind kicked up swirling dust devils and sent them dancing like dervishes along the barren yellow earth as far as the naked eye could see.

Some miles back, Barbara had decided she hated the area she'd driven through since leaving Pecos in mid-morning. The highway was virtually deserted. The heat rays lent an undulating effect to the roadway. Barbara had the uneasy sensation that she was driving directly into the mouth of hell.

*What was she doing in this godforsaken place any-
way?*

The question was not only startling, it was unnerving. Was the heat beginning to scramble her brains?
Barbara sliced a glance at the rearview mirror, sighing
with relief at the spark of amusement that glowed in the
bright hazel eyes reflecting back from the small rectan-
gle of glass. Those intelligent eyes mocked her with their
knowledge; of course they knew what she was doing
there—she was responding to a silent cry for help from
the only living relative she had left on this earth.

But why did she have to be in this particular piece of
unfriendly nothingness called West Texas? Barbara
complained mutely. If her aunt had to blaze a trail into
eccentricity, why couldn't she have chosen to do it
through the mountains of New England? Hadn't those
same mountains nurtured Ellie Holcomb through her
youth?

Well, actually, Barbara really had no idea how well
those mountains had nurtured her Aunt Ellie, since the
fiery, independent woman had shaken the rich New
England soil from her shoes years before Barbara was
born.

With nothing before her, and an equal amount of
nothing behind her, Barbara's mind escaped the blast
furnace of the present by recalling stories of the past.

The past was comprised of the years Barbara's father, Mark, and his older sister, Ellie, were growing up
in the small town in New Hampshire where Barbara was
born. On reflection, she could empathize with Ellie's
precipitous flight at age nineteen. By the time Barbara
had reached a similar age, she had found the town
deadly dull, too. Barbara had also bid a dry-eyed farewell to New Hampshire. But there the similarity be-

tween them had ended. Where Ellie had headed west in search of adventure, Barbara had headed to New York City for a career in modeling.

Until recently Barbara had succeeded in her chosen field beyond her wildest imaginings. It was not until now that she paused to wonder if her aunt had found the adventure she'd sought.

Adventure? Here? Lord! Squinting, Barbara's eyes swept the terrain with an encompassing glance. Other than the mountain ranges in the distance, the unvarying monotony of the landscape was depressing and a strain to the eyes, even through dark sunglasses. What sort of adventure could one possibly encounter in this vast wasteland? she reflected wryly.

Of course, like every other child her age, Barbara had grown up on Western movies and TV serials. For a few years before she entered her teens, shoot-'em-up, bang-bang shows were her favorite viewing fare. Following the hero of the moment, she thrilled vicariously as the "good guy" led the search for the bank robbers, stalked the dastardly villain who was terrorizing a small dusty town with his hired guns, and, with Stetson pulled low, rode into the twilit dusk, never to be heard from again. But, the silent, lone rider went by the boards when she discovered that boys were occasionally something other than a pain in the neck.

Since Barbara also believed that most legend was based on fact, she realized that the west had seen some pretty wild days. She was also convinced that the wild days were long gone. The only adventure she could imagine in this hot, dry place was the challenge to keep from being bored to distraction. And the letter she'd received from her aunt the week before appeared to prove her theory.

Ellie Holcomb's letter could not have come at a more crucial time in Barbara's life. After ten years of exceptional success, and grueling hard work in the field of modeling, she was tired—tired of eating lettuce leaves, carrot sticks, and the occasional, miniscule piece of broiled steak to maintain her ultra-slim figure; tired of attending dancersize classes to reinforce the calorie-less diet; tired of sleeping at least nine hours every night to stave off the signs of age; tired of the endless dash to get from one assignment to another. But, most of all, she was tired of the posturing, fawning men with their visions of a night spent with a cover girl.

"Come on, sweetheart, move! Push out that bottom lip. Look sexy and ready, will ya? Let's see more thigh."

The refrain ran through Barbara's mind; how often had she heard it, or one of its variations, over the last ten years? Grimacing, she groped for a cigarette from the package on the seat beside her, lighting it with relish. Although her agent had badgered and pleaded with her about quitting, smoking was the one pleasure Barbara absolutely refused to deny herself.

Drawing deeply on the filter-tipped cigarette, she released the smoke slowly as she mentally reread her aunt's letter.

I'm not getting around as spryly as before, Ellie wrote in her spidery scrawl. *This damned broken hip has slowed me down a mite.*

Broken hip! Barbara had thought with alarm. When had Ellie broken her hip? Anxiously, she had continued to read.

And, as I'm the only woman on the place, Ellie went on, *the inside of the house is beginning to resemble a pigsty.*

The only woman on the place? Barbara was appalled. Her aunt couldn't possibly manage alone. Why, she might even fall again and cause herself further injury! A possibility Ellie had brought up in her very next sentence.

I tripped over a tear in the carpet yesterday morning. I guess I'll just have to be careful of that ragged edge the next time I dust the parlor.

The parlor? Barbara had frowned over the word. She hadn't realized there were people who still referred to the living room or family room as "the parlor." And why was Aunt Ellie even attempting to dust the blasted room? Barbara's frown had turned into a self-mocking grimace. Aunt Ellie was attempting to dust the room *because* she was the only woman on the place!

This situation can't go on, Barbara had decided as she'd skimmed the remaining lines of her aunt's letter. *Now, dear, you take care of yourself, you hear? And don't concern yourself with your old aunt. I'm sure I'll find somebody to lug groceries to the ranch before I run out of supplies entirely.*

Her elderly aunt was running out of supplies? Barbara was horrified—and ensnared. Clutching the lined notebook paper in her fingers, she had hurried to the phone, her decision made; she would go to Texas to care for her aunt immediately upon completing her current modeling assignment!

Dan Greenberg, Barbara's agent, had been less than enthusiastic.

"Babsy! Are you out of your mind?" Dan had exploded. "You absolutely cannot afford to be away from

the action at this point in your career! You're not getting any younger, you know!''

As Barbara was all too aware of the encroaching
years—and competition—Dan's remark did little to
endear him to her. But, before she'd formed a protest,
he had managed to heap more fuel on the fire he'd
sparked.

"I mean," Dan had continued in a pleading tone,
"you're beginning to slip already! *I* have to work my
butt off now to get you jobs!''

Barbara's response to Dan had been short, succinct
and unprintable.

He has to work his butt off! Renewed anger coursed
through her. If Dan thought he'd been working hard the
last year or so, what did he think she was doing? Barbara fumed. She sure as the devil hadn't sat around
popping chocolates into her mouth! Oh, no! *She'd* been
running around like an idiot, merely to stay in place!

Barbara derived a tiny measure of enjoyment by repeating the short, succinct, unprintable expletive she'd
flung over the phone at Dan before hanging up on him,
adding furiously, ''And if he ever calls me Babsy again
I'll fire him!''

She didn't mean it, not really. Dan had been a
staunch supporter since the first day of her career. But
she was running scared—alarmed by the fact that she
was secretly tired of the rat race as well as dismayed with
the realization that, for Barbara Holcomb, modeling
assignments were no longer thick on the ground.

Concentrating on her thoughts, Barbara nearly
missed seeing the man lying on the dusty verge border-
ing the road, utilizing the scant shade provided by a
bluff that rose above the highway.

"What the—" Barbara blinked as she drew abreast of the sprawled form, continuing on for several yards before stamping on the brake pedal. Her reflex action caused the small car to skid out of control for breathtaking seconds. As the back end of the car fishtailed, she fought the wheel frantically, turning it into the direction of the skidding motion. When she finally brought the car to a shuddering stop, she was facing the opposite direction.

Thoroughly shaken, she sat absolutely still, her fingers welded to the wheel in a death grip. When the shudders of aftershock had subsided to tremors, and her breathing grew deeper than labored little gasps, she forced her eyes to focus on the catalyst of her near accident.

Appearing remarkably comfortable, the man was half sitting, half lounging in the dirt, his back supported by the gently sloping wall of the bluff. Peering at him through the dust-coated windshield, Barbara could understand why she'd almost missed seeing him; his tan attire blended into the yellow-brown color of the landscape.

But what was he doing there? Barbara gnawed her lip and narrowed her eyes on the supine form. The wide brim of his tan Stetson was pulled low on his forehead, concealing most of his face. As far as she could tell, he hadn't moved as much as a hair since she'd brought the car to a stop facing him.

Was he unconscious? she wondered uneasily. Or was he feigning unconsciousness, attempting to trap an unwary motorist?

What to do? Barbara released the door catch and swung the door open even as she advised herself to turn the vehicle around and get out of there as quickly as possible. Every sense alert to the possibility of danger, she approached the prone figure as cautiously as a young doe approaching a seemingly deserted stream.

"I gather that you're a fan of the famous Texan, A.J. Foyt?"

The low, roughly exciting male voice stopped Barbara in her tracks—physically and mentally.

"What . . . ? Who?" she demanded in an uncertain tone.

"I refer to your about-face stop there." He raised one arm to motion languidly at her car with a long-fingered hand. "And one of the greatest broad-sliders of them all."

"Broad-sliders?" Her frown betraying her utter confusion, she stepped closer to him. "What in the world is a broad-slider?"

"I can see you're not an auto racing fan." The man's tone was pitying. "A broad-slider is an expert on the oval dirt racetrack. A.J. Foyt was one of the best."

"Oh. I see." Barbara's jaws came together, snapping off her last word. Was she mad? In consternation, she measured the less than two feet of Texas earth that separated her from the sexy-voiced man. And, this close to him, her own eyes confirmed the fact that his body lived up to the promise of his voice!

Barbara took one careful step back. "Are you, ah, hurt in some way?" she asked nervously, shifting her glance in search of a disabled vehicle.

"Yeah." The man nodded. "My leg's a bit unsteady at the moment."

Which must be the reason why he hadn't moved, Barbara assured herself bracingly. Knowing full well there was no other vehicle but her own in sight, she again skimmed her glance over the unfriendly terrain.

"Umm...ahmm...have you had an accident?" The question sounded ridiculous, even to her own ears.

"Fell off my horse, ma'am," he drawled deeply.

"Really? How terrible!" Barbara's exclamation of sympathy was genuine. "Do you think your leg's broken?" Her eyes narrowed suspiciously at his short bark of laughter. "Did I say something amusing?" She arched her brows disdainfully.

"Oh, God, a greenhorn!" The Stetson moved as he shook his head. "I didn't fall off my horse, and my leg's not broken." A grin split his shadowed lips. "I was tugging on yours." Raising his arm, he swept the hat from his head as he went on tiredly, "I have a bullet hole in my thigh."

When she thought about it after, Barbara wasn't sure what shocked her more—the information that he'd been shot, or the startling male beauty of his facial features. To say the man was handsome would have been a deplorable understatement!

"A bull—" Barbara had to pause to moisten her suddenly parched lips. "You say you have a bullet hole in your leg?" While she carefully enunciated, she carefully took another step back.

"Right." His head dipped sharply in the affirmative.

As wary as she now was, Barbara couldn't avoid admiring the perfection of his looks. His bone structure was elegantly patrician. His lips were neither too thin nor too full. His eyes were so deep a brown they appeared almost black. The hair of the neatly trimmed, full mustache on his upper lip, and the mass that covered his exquisitely shaped head in the form of sweat-tousled curls, glinted like white gold. His skin was the shade of burnished copper that only certain blondes get when exposed to the unrelenting rays of the sun. Barbara personally knew many male models who would happily kill to have the sun-kissed, burnished look of this man.

"How did it get there?" Barbara inquired as her gaze took inventory of his appearance.

"Well, I certainly didn't shoot myself, lady." The corners of his lips tilted in a chiding smile. "The man who thought to use me for target practice is on the other side of this bluff."

Barbara's startled glance sliced to the looming overhang of earth. "Th—there's a man up there with a gun?" she croaked, taking another step back.

"Steady, lady," he advised, his crooning tone at variance with the twitch of amusement stirring the white-gold mustache. "I assure you he's harmless."

"But how can you be certain?" Barbara whispered shakily.

"Because he's dead."

Barbara had the oddest sensation that all the blood had drained from her body. Dead? The man was dead? Oh, God! She had seen the drunks and addicts dead-to-the-world unconscious in the subways and on the streets of New York and numerous other cities. Though the unsavory sight had disturbed her, it had not actually frightened her. The idea of a man, any man, lying dead, here and now, on the far side of the bluff, was a different story altogether.

"How did he get dead?" Intent on widening the distance between them, Barbara was unaware of the shrill edge to her tone and the ungrammatical form of her question; she was also beyond noticing the spasm of long-suffering playing briefly over the injured man's handsome face.

"I shot him."

It was as she'd feared, yet the very simplicity of his statement sent her reeling. She couldn't really be standing here conversing with a murderer? It wasn't possible—was it?

"God! Don't faint, lady!" His movements awkward, stiff, Thack heaved himself to his feet, a tired moan wrenched from his throat, a disgusted mutter held in check by his compressed lips. Why me? he asked in bleak silence, willing the woman to remain on her feet until he could hobble to her.

His leg ached like hell. Half dragging the injured limb, arms extended to catch her if she crumbled, Thack approached her. The fear and panic that widened her eyes and washed her face of color stopped his ungainly advance. Damn! She's terrified, he realized abruptly.

"Don't be afraid, lady!" Thack pleaded, his tone sharper than he'd intended. "I'm a lawman!"

"Lawman?"

Though uncertainty tinged her response, the I've-got-to-get-away-from-here look eased from her strained features. And they were extremely attractive features, too, even better up close than from the distance of several feet. Always one to appreciate the sight of a good-looking woman, Thack took enjoyment from the view before answering.

Her face was beautiful—not ravishingly or stunningly so—but beautiful just the same and, Thack frowned inwardly, vaguely familiar. The hair pulled away from her face and arranged into a loose knot at the crown of her head was a deep dark brown, shot through with streaks of red. His eye movement practiced and barely discernable, Thack skimmed her body. She was tall, five foot eight or nine, he judged, and ultra-slim, a trifle too slim for his taste. But her legs were long, slender and, from the portion he could see from the hem of her cotton wraparound skirt, shaped to entice a man's hand.

Thack experienced a sudden itching in his palm to explore the flesh concealed by the brightly patterned skirt. Sighing over the necessity to deny the itch, his swiftly moving gaze noted her neatly rounded hips, tucked-in waist and lamentably small breasts.

Barely enough there to fill a broad palm, he decided, ending his perusal by raising his eyes to stare into the shocked, hazel depths of hers.

"Yes, ma'am, a lawman," Thack responded at length.

Wariness emanated from her like a palpable force field. "You're not in uniform." Despite its softness, her tone held accusation.

Thack sighed; he was getting damned tired of balancing on one leg. "I'm a Texas Ranger, ma'am," he informed her wearily. "Rangers have no official uniform, we wear our own clothes." Lifting his hand, he dipped his fingers into his shirt pocket. "See?" he asked as he withdrew his identification. "The name's Thackery Sharp," he added. "Thack to my friends. You can check me out in Sanderson," he hesitated, "*if* we ever get there."

"Is Sanderson the nearest town?"

"Yes, ma'am." Thack closed his eyes for an instant. Damn! Would this woman never be satisfied? If he didn't sit down, and soon, he was afraid he'd humiliate himself by falling down. A twitch of a smile touched his lips; falling down is poor form for a Ranger!

"Something amuses you, Mr. Sharp?"

"No, ma'am." Thack controlled his lips—and the urge to laugh at her formality. Not Thack or even Thackery, but Mr. Sharp! *That should tell me where I stand!* "That wasn't a smile you detected on my lips, it was a grimace of pain. Would you mind if I sat down? In the car, maybe?"

"Oh! Oh, heaven's I'm sorry!" A flush of embarrassment crept from her throat to her invitingly soft-looking cheeks. "Certainly! Of course you may sit down in the car!"

"I do appreciate it, ma'am," Thack murmured somberly, swallowing a grin as he hobbled to the small vehicle.

Thack's amusement with his less than enthusiastic rescuer dissipated rapidly as he struggled to fold his six-foot-four-inch frame into the sports car's less than roomy interior.

"Oh, Lord!" The between-the-teeth mutter shivered on the air-conditioner-cooled air as he gripped his thigh and attempted to stretch the injured leg out straight. "Can you move this seat back at all?" Thack groaned.

"Oh, jeez, I'm sorry!"

Thack let his head fall against the headrest on the back of the seat as she scrambled into the car and fumbled with a lever at the side of her seat. A gratified sigh whooshed through his lips as the seat eased back a few inches and the angry pounding in his thigh subsided to a rhythmic throb.

"Better?" Anxiety underscored the word.

"Infinitely." Turning his head to her, Thack dredged up a smile. "The cool air feels good, too. I estimate I was lying out there for nearly an hour. September in Texas can be damned hot."

"I'll say!" A flashing grin transformed her face.

Thack caught his breath at the change in her features. Where before she'd appeared merely moderately beautiful, the animation of amusement lent a glow to her face that was downright demoralizing. Thack sighed in resignation as the throb in his leg was echoed by another in the lower half of his body. Staring down at the less intimate portion of his body that was throbbing painfully, Thack contemplated the corresponding portion.

Hell, he mused dejectedly, he didn't even know her name. And she sure as tomorrow didn't trust him. *Why me?* The mute protest rang inside his head.

"Are . . . are you all right?" Her voice gave evidence to the renewal of her fear.

Cracking the lids he'd lowered in self-defense to a mere slit, Thack gazed at her broodingly.

"Sure." He tried a smile on for size; it didn't fit very well. "Do you want to dance?" Thack mentally shrugged as he watched her eyebrows draw together in a frown of confusion; maybe someday he'd learn to control his offbeat sense of humor—and his mouth!

"How can you joke at a time like this?" she demanded angrily.

"Because crying plays hell with my tough, lawman image," he retorted. He exhaled wearily when she stared back at him blankly. "Could we go now?" Thack requested politely. "I mean, before this hole in my leg starts bleeding again?"

The anxiety was back in her eyes again, only this time it was anxiety *for* him, not *about* him.

"Oh, dear," she moaned contritely. "I am sorry. Is there anything I can do?"

"You could drive," Thack suggested laconically.

"Yes. Of course. I will!"

Biting the inside of his lip to keep from laughing aloud at her flustered stuttering, Thack regarded her solemnly. Man! She was more appealing than a pure-bred Arabian filly! An erotic vision of her, sans wrap-around skirt and flower-splashed blouse, swam into his mind to tease his senses and torment his body. The ache radiating to every nerve ending in his body was startling in its intensity. Thack couldn't remember the last time he'd ached this badly for a woman. And he was wounded and hurting!

Ol' son, you have definitely been in the West Texas hills too long, Thack chastised himself dryly. The time has come for a short break. He cast a hooded glance at the woman beside him. Come to that, he mused, maybe it's time for a long break. But, first things first. Before you can go courting, it helps if you have a name and address. The woman obligingly supplied the former as he opened his mouth to ask.

"I'm Barbara Holcomb, by the way." She turned her head to flash a smile at him before turning her attention back to the highway.

"Hello Barbara Holcomb." Thack's responding smile gave way to a contemplative frown. Holcomb? Could she possibly be related to Ellie in some way?

"What—what about that man—" she jerked her head slightly "—back there?" Barbara bit her lip in agitation.

"He's not going anywhere," Thack pointed out lazily; Lord, the cool air swirling around his sweaty body felt good!

"Well, I know that!" Barbara slanted an irate glance at him. "What I mean is, why did you shoot him?"

"Since he was firing at me, it seemed like a reasonable idea to fire back." Thack lifted one shoulder fatalistically. "I was a better shot."

Barbara sighed. "I was trying to find out why you were pursuing him in the first place. What had he done?"

"Some two-bit cattle rustling." Thack shook his head in wonder. "Hell, I had no idea the guy was even armed. He paid a high price for a few head of beef."

"I didn't realize there were any cattle rustlers left in this day and age." Barbara looked amazed. "I was envisioning a very dull visit to this desolate-looking country."

"You're visiting?" Thack perked up considerably. "Around here?"

"Ummm." Barbara shifted her eyes from the hypnotic monotony of the road. "I'm on my way to care for my aunt. She has a ranch outside of Sanderson."

"Your aunt is Ellie Holcomb?" Thack sat up alertly.

Barbara shot a surprised grin his way. "Why, yes. Do you know my Aunt Ellie?"

"Hell, everybody in these parts knows Ellie." Thack grinned back. "She's a fine woman. A little eccentric maybe, but a damned fine woman."

Barbara laughed easily. "That's Aunt Ellie, all right. The way I understand it, she was *always* eccentric, even as a teenager."

The chuckle tickling Thack's throat subsided as something Barbara had said registered in his mind. "Did you say you were visiting to *care* for Ellie?" At her affirmative nod, he probed further. "Why should Ellie need care? Is she sick?"

"No, not exactly." Barbara shook her head, which caused a strand of gleaming hair to be dislodged from her topknot. It slid down her exposed neck and formed into a loose curl. Thack had to fight a sudden urge to reach out and stroke the chestnut lock, and the skin it nestled against. His hand was moving when the sound of her voice arrested him.

"Her letter to me was sketchy," Barbara continued. "But apparently she had a fall and broke her hip."

"And old Frank's not there to help her," Thack muttered under his breath.

"I beg your pardon?" Barbara sliced a quizzical look at him.

"Nothing." Thack smiled. "Go on."

"She informed me in her letter that there's no other woman on the place." Barbara's tone took on a hint of amazement. "I mean, really! How in the world can she manage without another woman there?"

"A lot of early settlers managed well enough," Thack opined in a dryly amused tone.

Barbara made a very unladylike sound. "Well, my aunt doesn't have to manage alone. That's why I'm here."

"From where?"

"What?" Barbara turned her head to frown at him.

"You're here from where?" Thack frowned back. "Where do you call home?"

"Oh." The crease on her forehead smoothed away. "I'm originally from New Hampshire, as is Aunt Ellie. But I've lived in New York City for ten years."

"Why?"

"Why what?"

"Why would you want to live in New York City?" Thack asked reasonably. "It's noisy and dirty and crime-ridden."

If truth be known, Barbara had muttered similar condemning words countless times. Yet, hearing it from this lazy-looking Texan put her back up. "New York City just happens to be the most exciting city in the world," she said repressively. "And I happen to work there."

"So there!" Thack retaliated in a childish, taunting tone. "And what sort of work do you do in this most wonderful of cities?" He went on conversationally, ignoring the explosive look she tossed him.

"I'm a model," she said grudgingly. Then, as if unable to let his earlier statement about crime in New York go, she added, "And I've never run across a dead man while doing it!"

"Just as I suspected, no excitement there at all." Thack forced himself to drawl the words as he drew slow breaths in an effort to combat the throb in his leg. "Sounds pretty dull to me."

As unobtrusively as possible, he slid his right hand down his thigh to test the big workman-style handkerchief he'd used as a bandage for signs of fresh wetness.

Barbara's sharp hazel eyes caught the movement of his hand.

"Is it bleeding?" she asked steadily, trying to remember how to stop a wound from bleeding.

"Yeah." Thack exhaled the word along with a harsh breath.

"Should I pull over and see if I can get it to stop?" Her foot eased off the gas pedal.

"No." Thack shook his head, and wet his lips. "We'll be in Sanderson in a few minutes. The doc there will fix it."

Frowning in consternation, he stared down at the small spot of red that was seeping through the material of his trousers.

Two

Frightened again, but this time *for* Thack not *of* him, Barbara fumbled with the now crumpled cigarette pack wedged beneath her thigh. What would she do if the wound in his leg began bleeding profusely? she worried, her fingers searching for the opening in the top of the pack. Distantly, she could see the town of Sanderson now, but would he be all right until she got him to a doctor? How long did it take for a person to bleed to death?

Panic was beginning to build when her spiraling thoughts and groping fingers were stilled by the sound of Thack's calm voice, and the gentleness of his hand as it covered hers.

"Don't you know that smoking's bad for you?"

"Who are you—the surgeon general?" Barbara snapped irritably, yanking her hand from his. "I *need* a cigarette, Mr. Sharp!"

Thack sighed. "You don't, you know." His gaze dropped to her trembling fingers. "Then again, maybe you do." Brushing her hand away from the pack, he shook a cigarette from it. "Running across me has kind'a rattled you, hasn't it?" With the ease of familiarity, he lit the cigarette, then reached across the console to place it between her lips.

"Thank you." As she drew in deeply, Barbara had the oddest sensation that she was drawing the taste of Thack into her body; never had a cigarette been so satisfying. Shying away from the strangely sensuous thought, she concentrated on his question.

"Yes, I'm feeling a little rattled." She smiled weakly. "Meeting a man with a bullet wound in his leg is hardly an everyday occurrence for me."

"Receiving a bullet wound in the leg is hardly an everyday occurrence for me, either." Thack's retort was followed by a grimace of disgust. "Or, for that matter, having my horse bolt away from me."

"Your horse?" Barbara arched her brows; that explained the absence of another vehicle.

"Yeah." Thack smiled sourly. "Jim Dandy bolted away from a rattler—the hammerhead."

Barbara groaned silently. A bullet wound, a dead man and a rattlesnake. Wonderful. Welcome to Texas, greenhorn!

"You're looking a mite green around the edges, Ms. Holcomb." All the dryness was gone from Thack's tone, leaving it sharply alert. "Are you feeling all right?"

Barbara stabbed the cigarette butt into the ashtray under the dash. "Yes, I'm fine." Shifting her gaze to avoid the intensity of his stare, she caught sight of the red stain beginning to spread over Thack's tan pant leg. This time she groaned aloud. "Oh, my God!"

"What is it?" Thack jerked erect in the seat. "What's the matter? Are you sick?"

Barbara could actually feel the laserlike probe of his eyes. "Your leg!" she blurted hoarsely. "Is it much farther to the doctor's office?"

"Oh, that." Thack flicked one hand with nerve-racking unconcern. "It's not all that much blood, Ms. Holcomb, and no, the doctor's not much farther." His hand moved again to indicate the fact that they were now entering the small town. "Turn right at the next intersection."

His calm manner made her feel foolish—which in turn made her angry. If he wasn't worried about bleeding to death, why should she get herself upset? Barbara railed. Her lips compressed, she followed his directions to a building with a small sign indicating an MD in residence. Thack placed a hand on her wrist as she moved to get out of the car.

"I can manage from here," he said softly. "Thank you for your help—" he paused briefly "—and your concern." His teeth flashed startling white against his coppery skin and, with a grunted curse, he swung his injured leg out of the car. Pausing again, he glanced back at her. "Give my best to your aunt." Quickly, concisely, he gave her directions to Ellie's property, then, levering his long body out of the car, he hobbled toward the doctor's office.

After Barbara had left the small town behind her, she realized that in her agitation she hadn't even looked at it. Strange, she mused, her gaze searching for the wooden sign marked *Holcomb* that Thack had told her to watch for. She had not missed as much as a hair on

Thack's head, yet she couldn't remember a single thing about Sanderson—except for the doctor's office.

A frown drew a faint line between her delicately arched eyebrows. It was more than strange, really. She rarely looked twice at any man... and with good reason!

Her soft lips twisting bitterly, Barbara forced her thoughts away from the male of the species—her pet antipathy—and back to the business at hand—that of locating the road that would lead to her aunt's house.

When she finally did spot the Holcomb sign, she sent out a silent thank-you to Thack. Without his precise directions, she probably would have missed the weather-beaten piece of board hanging crookedly from a precariously leaning post at the entrance to the narrow dirt road.

The small car bounced jarringly over the rutted road that was actually little more than a dirt track. Relief vied with dismay inside Barbara as she brought the car to a halt in front of the house. This gray clapboard structure was her aunt's home? Barbara sighed as her dulled gaze surveyed the dismal appearance of the building. *This* was the haven her aunt referred to in her letters as her "little slice of heaven?"

Shaking her head sadly, Barbara pushed the car door open and stepped onto the hard-baked earth. The dry heat slammed into her like a physical blow. Lord! If this was Ellie's idea of heaven, she shuddered to think what her aunt's concept of hell would be!

For a moment Barbara's shoulders drooped dejectedly. She just knew the house was without air-conditioning. Then, rolling her shoulders to work out the stiffness in her back, she straightened her spine. She'd get used to the heat, she assured herself; she had no choice.

After retrieving her purse from the car, she swung the door shut and strode toward the house. As she approached the three unstable-looking steps that rose to a verandalike porch, Barbara's gaze was snared by a blurred movement on the other side of the screened door.

"Is that you, Babs?" Hope and delight mingled in the husky voice that could be heard through the screen.

"Yes. Aunt Ellie?" Barbara smiled as she gingerly mounted the steps; just as her agent was the only person to call her Babsy, her aunt was the sole person to call her Babs. Barbara rather liked the latter nickname. The door swung inward as she crossed the porch.

"Well, a'course it's Aunt Ellie! You get on in here and give your old aunt a hug, darlin'."

Stepping over the threshold, Barbara blinked to adjust her vision from the glare of the sunlight to the dim interior of the house. Her tall, sharply angular body supported by crutches, Ellie stood just inside the door, her worn face alight with pleasure.

"Should you be on your feet?" Barbara exclaimed in concern, circling the older woman's waist to bestow a gentle hug. As she moved back, her gaze swept the plaster cast that encased Ellie's right leg from her knee to her foot, ending where her toes began.

As Barbara's gaze drifted the length of the smudged, graying plaster, her eyes narrowed with suspicion. Since when is a cast applied to the lower leg to immobilize a broken hip? she wondered wryly, raising her glance to her aunt's shifting eyes and flushed face.

"Ah. Ah-hem." Ellie cleared her throat.

"Yes?" Barbara prodded gently.

"Ah, yes, well, my hip's not broke."

"Really!" Barbara's eyebrows peaked over sparkling eyes.

Handling the crutches adroitly, Ellie swung her body around. "Come into the kitchen and sit down." She tossed the invitation over her shoulder as she propelled her body across the sparsely furnished living room. "I'll explain over a cup of coffee."

Her emotions tugging sympathetically, Barbara trailed Ellie into the surprisingly bright kitchen. Pausing in the doorway, her eyes widened with delight. The room was long and narrow. Gleaming white appliances and modern wood cabinets set off walls painted a buttery yellow. The abundance of hanging green plants gave the room a deceptively cool, springlike ambience.

"How do you take your coffee?"

Snapped out of her thoughts by Ellie's query, Barbara was about to reply, but she suddenly stopped herself. With an impish smile lighting her face, she decided to forego drinking her coffee calorie-free black—at least for the duration of her visit.

"With cream and sugar," she responded with relish. "But wait!" Belatedly coming to her senses, Barbara strode into the room, shaking her head at both herself and her aunt. "*I'll* get the coffee. You get off that leg!"

With a show of meekness that Barbara knew was contrary to her aunt's nature, Ellie thumped her way to a wooden, ladder-back chair painted a glistening white, waving a hand dismissively as Barbara moved to help her.

"I can still get in and out of a chair, honey!" Ellie grumbled, hiding a grin. "You just pour the coffee into the cups I set out. Oh, and bring that coffee cake there on the counter. It's fresh. I baked it this morning."

Coffee, cream, sugar, *and* the ingredients for coffee cake? Barbara frowned as she poured the dark brew from the old-fashioned stove-top pot into the large white mugs. Hadn't Ellie mentioned something in her letter about running out of supplies? Umm. There was definitely the scent of a red herring in West Texas!

Completing the small task of serving the coffee, Barbara slid into the matching chair opposite Ellie. Inhaling deeply, she sighed in relief as the moist steam banished the hot smell from her nostrils and the rich aroma of coffee replaced the arid scent of the outdoors.

"Heavenly."

Barbara wasn't even aware that she'd murmured the comment aloud until her aunt gave a gleeful bark of laughter. Inhaling again, she returned Ellie's chuckle.

"Well, after that ghastly drive, this really is heavenly." Barbara smiled apologetically. "I'm sorry, Aunt Ellie, but I'm afraid I find your section of Texas both too dry and too desolate."

"West Texas has to grow on a body." Ellie shrugged her unconcern. "By the time you have to leave, you'll likely be aching to stay."

Though she seriously doubted her aunt's statement, Barbara prudently kept her opinion to herself. Then the tang of cinnamon teased her taste buds as Ellie sliced into the coffee cake.

"If you think the smell of my coffee's heavenly, wait till you wrap your teeth around this." Transferring a large wedge of the cake to a small plate, Ellie slid it across the table to Barbara.

"Oh, I really shouldn't." Her hazel eyes filling with a longing that spanned her ten-year career, Barbara stared at temptation dressed in the guise of an innocent piece of cake. The inner battle was brief—temptation won hands down. Ignoring the scolding voice of her conscience, she lifted the fork beside the plate and dug into the cake with childlike gusto.

When the plate had been cleaned of its last golden crumb, Barbara slid the crumpled cigarette pack from her handbag, mildly surprised when her aunt accepted a cigarette from the proffered pack.

"That was absolutely the very best coffee cake I've ever tasted." Barbara offered the compliment as she lighted first her aunt's cigarette and then her own with a disposable lighter.

"And even more satisfying when followed by a good smoke." Ellie drew on the cigarette, then frowned slightly. "Even though I do prefer the unfiltered kind."

A faraway look clouded Barbara's eyes. "He said it was bad for my health."

"He?" Ellie's frown darkened. "Who the devil is *he*?"

Aware that she had once again murmured her thoughts aloud, Barbara smiled. "Oh, a man I met along the roadside."

Ellie's face paled. "A man you met along the roadside," she repeated flatly, then her voice cracked. "Barbara Holcomb! You didn't stop to pick up a hitchhiker?"

"No, of course not!" Barbara exclaimed. "At least, not exactly." Thinking about Thack brought his image to her mind; even with her feelings about men in general, she had to admit that he certainly was one of *the* most attractive men she'd ever seen!

"Then what, exactly, did happen?" Ellie demanded hoarsely, visibly upset by the contemplative expression on her niece's face.

Attempting to calm her aunt, Barbara briefly described her encounter with the wounded man. "I assure you there is no reason for you to be concerned." If Barbara had thought her explanation was sufficient she was in for a shock. Her aunt nearly exploded.

"A wounded man! And you alone on a deserted highway!" Ellie was actually sputtering. "Barbara, who was he?"

"His name is Thackery Sharp. He said he's a Texas Ranger."

The change in Ellie was immediate and startling. Warm color suffused her weather-roughened cheeks and her faded blue eyes took on a soft glow.

"Thack."

Even though her aunt's murmur could hardly be called a question Barbara responded to it. "Yes, Thack. Do you know him?"

The smile that moved over Ellie's lips was every bit as soft as the glow in her eyes. "I'd judge that just about everybody in West Texas knows Thack Sharp. That boy does get around."

Boy? Thack? Barbara's exquisitely molded mouth quirked with a grin. Not by a long shot! Thackery Sharp was definitely not a *boy*! A delicate shudder tiptoed down her spine. Her tone was amazingly steady. "Mr. Sharp didn't strike me as a boy at all."

Ellie's full-throated laughter added luster to the bright room. "It's just an expression, honey. But you're right. In anybody's estimation, Thack is *el macho hombre*!"

Very much a virile man, Barbara translated mutely. Yes. Oh, yes indeed, Thack was decidedly *el macho hombre*—and then some! The shudder down her spine intensified. Uncomfortable with her reaction to the mere mention of his name, Barbara felt grateful when Ellie's brisk tone scattered her wandering thoughts.

"You said Thack was wounded!" Her bushy gray-tinged brows came together over the bridge of her long, but straight, nose. "Is the wound serious?"

"In my opinion, *any* bullet wound is serious!" Barbara shivered. "But Thack insisted it was not." Remembered amazement widened her eyes. "The wound was bleeding enough to stain his pant leg yet he seemed unconcerned. I'll admit, it scared the hell out of me!"

Ellie laughed softly and patted Barbara's hand reassuringly. "Thack knows best, honey. If he said it wasn't serious, it probably wasn't." Lifting her cup, she drank the last of the coffee before holding it out beseechingly. "I'd love a refill," she prodded.

Barbara jumped to her feet. "Of course!" Crossing to the stove she scooped up a hot pad, then brought the pot to the table. "I'll have another myself." As she poured the dark brew into the cups, a line of consternation creased her smooth brow. "You know, I can't believe I'm sitting in this heat drinking hot coffee—of all things! At home I'd be gulping down mineral water with a dash of lime."

"Mineral water!" Ellie made a sour face. "Ugh. I'll take my caffeine, thank you."

A teasing smile tilted the corners of Barbara's lips. "I wonder if Thack disapproves of caffeine as well as nicotine?" she mused aloud.

"Thack?" Ellie nearly choked on the coffee. "Thack guzzles coffee like he's afraid the government was about to place a ban on it or something." Her eyes narrowed. "Come to that, he always smoked like a barn on fire, too. Fact is, Thack was the last person I'd 'uv expected to quit. Why, Thack's always been the first to admit to being addicted to the three c's.''

A sensation of unease unfurled in the pit of Barbara's stomach. Coffee, cigarettes and . . . cocaine? She shivered as her thoughts tumbled sickeningly. Was Thack's laid-back attitude drug induced? Was the use of drugs the reason for his seeming unconcern for the wound in his leg? She hadn't noticed the betraying evidence in his eyes, but then, except for a few minutes, he'd had his eyes shaded by the wide brim of his hat.

Barbara had reason to abhor the use of drugs; she'd witnessed the destructive effects on one of her friends. Surprised at the depth of disappointment she felt, she stared moodily into her cup. Her head jerked up at her aunt's indulgent chuckle.

''I swear, Thack consumes more chocolate than the average ten-year-old.''

''Chocolate!'' Barbara's voice cracked from the relief trembling through her; she didn't know why it should matter so very much, and at the moment she was too distracted to wonder about it. ''Thack is a chocoholic?'' The laughter that bubbled from her throat felt good.

''The worst.'' Ellie laughed with her. ''And particular, too. He doesn't like just any ol' chocolate; he likes *good* chocolate.'' Her faded eyes danced with inner amusement. ''There's many a time Thack's requested chocolate as a reward for a favor done.''

Confused, Barbara frowned. ''Payment for a favor? I don't understand.''

''Well, I'll grant that Thack isn't the easiest man *to* understand.'' Ellie shook her head. ''He's a fine lawman; one of the best. But he's a damn sight more than that, too. Seems to touch more places than the wind. A body finds himself short on help and long on repairs, out of nowhere Thack comes a'ridin', ready to set to at fixin' most anything from broken corral rails to holes in the roof. That horse of his ain't no slouch at working cattle either." A soft smile curved Ellie's thin lips. "And, without fail, when payment is offered, Thack answers, 'Next time you're in town, just leave some chocolate at the sheriff's office for me.' And they always do."

"Town? Do you mean Sanderson?"

"Wherever, honey. The town closest to wherever they happen to be at the time." Ellie smiled chidingly. "I do recollect telling you that just about everybody in West Texas knows Thack."

"Well, yes," Barbara grinned. "But I hardly thought you meant literally."

"Child, I meant literally," Ellie grinned back.

Mulling over her aunt's words, Barbara grew quiet. It would appear that Thack was something of a local hero. Strangely, she was not surprised at all; Thack certainly did look the part—with all that white-gold hair and bronzed handsomeness. But the chocoholic bit really blew her mind! Barbara stifled a burst of laughter. That man had to be in his mid-thirties! Too much!

Barbara's amusement was short-lived. "He shot a man, you know?" she said with sudden starkness.

Ellie sobered instantly. "Thack did? Where—when?"

As briefly as possible, Barbara told her aunt the parts she'd left out of her original explanation. "And Thack seemed so unconcerned about it," she finished, unsuccessfully trying to suppress a shudder.

Ellie studied Barbara's expression for a long, quiet moment. "What bothers you, honey?" she asked shrewdly. "The fact that the man was dead or that Thack seemed unconcerned?"

"Both, I suppose." Barbara sighed. "I...I liked Thack, but I'm having a problem dealing with his casual attitude about taking a human life."

"Honey, Thack's a lawman. A lawman who takes his work very seriously." Ellie frowned. "Didn't you say he fired in self-defense?"

"Yes, but—"

"No buts," Ellie interrupted. "If Thack said that, you can believe it. I've never heard of Thack being caught in a lie; he simply never lies." She chuckled. "He's probably too lazy to be bothered. And, as far as him being casual, don't be fooled. I think Thack's made up of mostly still water," she grinned. "And you do know what they say about still water—don't you?"

"It runs deep," Barbara responded automatically, thoughtfully.

"Exactly." Ellie rested her case with a satisfied smile.

Drifting back into her thoughts, Barbara absently began clearing the table. Memory stirred as she placed what was left of the coffee cake on the counter next to the sink. What was it about the cake? Oh, yes—supplies! Compressing her lips to control a smile, she turned to level an innocent look at her aunt.

"I think I'll bring in my suitcases," she said consideringly, "but leave the unpacking until I get back from Sanderson."

"Sanderson?" Ellie blinked. "What do you want in Sanderson?"

"Didn't you mention something in your letter about running out of supplies?" She lifted one delicately arched brow.

Dark color spread up and under the deep tan on Ellie's cheeks. "Ah, yes, well," she cleared her throat with a rattling sound. "Ah, I kind'a exaggerated the situation."

"Kind'a?" Losing control over her stern expression, Barbara smiled softly.

Ellie smiled back tentatively. "I was hurt and lonely, honey. I'm not by myself on the place. I have two hired men—old and crochety as they are." Her sigh tugged at Barbara's heart. "I . . . I got to longing for family." She blinked fiercely, as if unused to the feel of tears. "And you and me, Babs, we're all we got anymore." Suddenly the flood gates opened and tears poured down her lined face.

"Oh, Aunt Ellie!" Her own eyes filling with tears, Barbara ran to Ellie, cradling her gaunt, trembling body close. "Don't you dare make me cry, it makes my mascara run!" Sniffling, she rocked back and forth, stroking her aunt's shoulders and arms. "I'm sorry I teased you. But, darling, you didn't need to exaggerate the situation at all. All you had to do was ask. I'd have come just the same."

Swiping at her face with trembling fingers, Ellie leaned back in the chair. "I'm an old fool," she said gruffly. "Crying like an abandoned baby."

"You're not a fool!" Barbara protested, groping through her bag for a tissue. "And you're the youngest *old* person I know." Locating the rather crumpled tissue, she handed it over with an apologetic smile. "And there's no shame in crying at times, either. It cleans out the tear ducts."

Ellie's sad expression was immediately lightened by a reminiscent smile. "Your father used to tell me that, more years ago than I care to remember."

"He used to tell me that, too." Barbara sighed.

"You still miss him, don't you, honey?"

Swallowing the lump in her throat, Barbara nodded. "I still miss both of them." She bit her bottom lip, then spoke aloud the cry that had rung in her mind for more than five years. "Why did I have to lose both my mother and father at the same time, Aunt Ellie? It isn't fair."

Now it was Ellie who was cradling Barbara's slender body. "A lot of life isn't fair, Babs. And a snowstorm, along with a curving road, is impervious to fairness. And, even though you were terribly hurt, it was best they went together. They were still as much in love as they were when they married, over twenty years before." Putting Barbara from her, Ellie smiled gently. "You know as well as I do that neither one of them probably would have lived very long without the other."

"I suppose so," Barbara agreed reluctantly. "But that doesn't make it hurt any less."

"I know, honey." With a final pat, Ellie became brisk. "Now, I think we'll get you settled in." Reaching behind her, she fumbled for the crutches she'd propped against the back of the chair.

"Aunt Ellie, don't you dare get up!" Jumping to her feet, Barbara whisked the crutches away from Ellie. "I insist you stay off that leg. Just point me in the right direction, and I'll settle myself in."

The right direction turned out to be a small, unpretentious room off the living room. Decorated in what Barbara secretly dubbed "early garage-sale," the room appealed to her simply because it had the same homey feeling that came from slipping into well-worn, comfortable slippers. As she hefted her large suitcase onto the bed, a gentle smile curved her lips. The feeling

stealing through her was unfamiliar yet recognizable—
the feeling was of homecoming.

The furniture had been used, but lovingly so. The
bedspread and the lacy curtains that covered the window without blocking the light were faded but spot-
lessly clean. A handwoven Indian rug in shades of
brown and startling white covered an area of the floor
beside the single bed.

Comfort. Sanctuary. Home.

Sanctuary? Barbara frowned over the odd, errant
thought. Had she subconsciously felt the need for
sanctuary? Well, perhaps. Sighing, she began transferring clothes from her case to the drawers of the old-
fashioned dresser and the one small closet.

Sanctuary. Yes, in a way she had been searching for
a refuge ever since she'd walked away from the luxury
of the expensive highrise apartment, and the man who'd
provided it, three years before.

Her actions automatic, she stashed the empty cases
under the bed and then sank onto it, too tired to fight
the image that rose to haunt her. Wincing, she closed
her eyes. Even after three years, merely thinking about
him hurt. The memory speared through the protective
layers she'd applied to the wound he'd inflicted.

Peter Vanzant. His name ripped through Barbara's
mind like a damaging wind. How she had loved him, or
thought she had. Urbane and sophisticated, Peter had
a reputation for being ruthless in business deals and
devastating in emotional situations.

And devastated was exactly how Barbara had felt
after ending her six-month affair with him.

How had she ever convinced herself she was different from any of the others? A bitter, derisive smile
pulled at her soft lips. It certainly wasn't as if she'd been

unaware of his reputation with women; she had been hearing gossip about his affairs for years before she actually met him. But, unlike Peter, she was incapable of separating her emotional response from her physical reaction.

From their very first meeting at that dreadfully dull party, he had utterly captivated her. Peter was the walking, talking answer to every young woman's dream of perfection. Tall, dark, broodingly handsome, Peter had the ability to make a woman's knees tremble with a simple penetrating stare. For Barbara the trembling reaction had spread through her entire body when he favored her with a smile that told her of his interest. She was a lost soul from that minute till the final break seven months later.

Even after she'd returned to full sanity, Barbara was amazed that she'd withstood the power of his lure for one full month. But, in the end, his patience paid off. She'd caved in completely, so completely that she broke rules she'd set up for herself and had adhered to rigidly before she met Peter. She agreed to live with him without the benefit of a legal commitment.

Ensconced in luxury, Barbara had managed to convince herself that Peter would come to love her as much as she loved him. Peter had made it extremely easy for her to convince herself. In an age of equal everything, including sexual experience, he had been genuinely thrilled by the discovery of her virginity.

Petted and indulged by an expert, Barbara had allowed herself to drift on the cloud of sensual passion Peter wove around her. Steeped in the glow of first love, first passion, it had required six months for the truth to sink in. Peter spoke the words of lovemaking beautifully, while never speaking the words of love.

Barbara had not run away from Peter like a thief in the night. While leaving all the expensive gifts he'd bought for her, she had packed her own things, then had sat down to wait for him.

At first Peter had been impatient with her; he'd spent the day in particularly annoying business negotiations. When it became clear that she was dead serious about leaving their "little nest" he grew angry, then coaxing. And when Peter coaxed he was hard to resist.

Not even to herself could Barbara ever claim that she hadn't been tempted to stay with him. In actual fact, she had longed to stay with him with every fiber of her being. Yet, with an inner strength she didn't know she possessed, she'd walked away from him. She had never looked back until now.

Sanctuary? Yes, perhaps that explained the urge that had sent her rushing headlong to this godforsaken piece of barrenness called West Texas. Though the love she'd felt for Peter had died months ago, the humiliation and shame of her own precipitous actions still lingered.

For Barbara, stung and still hurting from it, there had been no other involvements, no other men. Though she didn't truly believe that all men were takers, she doubted her own astuteness at distinguishing the takers from the sharers. Determined not to be emotionally devastated again, she kept her distance from the male of the species.

Three

"Babs? Honey, there's hot water if you want to freshen up before supper. The bathroom's at the end of the hall."

Startled out of her reverie, Barbara's head snapped up. Supper? Good heaven's! Had she been sitting and brooding *that* long? Blinking, she glanced at the pretty digital watch on her slender wrist as the numbers pulsed to five-fifteen. No, she hadn't been thinking about the past for that long. Smiling ruefully, she got to her feet and walked to the door; in New York she never ate dinner—or supper—before seven.

"Will twenty minutes be okay, Aunt Ellie?" she called.

"That'll be fine, honey," Ellie shouted back. "Take your time."

Consigning Peter Vanzant to where he belonged, her past, Barbara gathered her toiletries and fresh clothes and headed for the antiquated bathroom, softly humming the melody of a current ballad.

Setting aside the ravished supper tray his landlady had delivered to him half an hour ago Thack shifted into a comfortable position on the narrow bed and crossed his arms under his head.

The painkillers the doctor had given him had reduced the throbbing in his thigh to a dull ache and, as long as he didn't move too suddenly, Thack could keep his mind from dwelling on the pain of the wound.

As of 4:00 P.M. that afternoon, Thack was officially on extended leave of absence. He didn't have a thing in the world he *had* to do. He was on vacation. A smile lifted the corners of his slightly sensuous lips. A vacation, moreover, that was some five years overdue. His time was his own. He could do any damn thing he felt like doing.

Thack felt like making love.

Savoring the fire slowly building deep inside, Thack chuckled softly. Making love was also long overdue! But, to be precise, Thack felt like making love to Barbara Holcomb.

"You've got a hole in your leg, Sharp." Full-throated laughter followed the muttered reminder. His body shifted with the rippling laughter, causing a shaft of pain to shoot through his thigh and a grunt of discomfort to escape through his now tight lips. "Goes with the hole in your head," he groaned derisively.

Still the fire of need spread to heat his entire body. A frown drew his white-gold brows together. What was it about Ellie's niece that intrigued him so? True, Barbara was more than passingly attractive. But over the years he'd met many attractive women, and most of them were willing—for anything. And yet he'd never felt the sexual immediacy he'd experienced that afternoon on encountering Barbara.

Strange. Thack's frown deepened. No matter how he searched his memory, he couldn't remember *ever* feeling that strong a response to a woman—not even his ex-wife!

With his bottom teeth, Thack gnawed on the silvery tips of his mustache. It was more than strange. It was damned weird! The warmth inside reached flash point and Thack shifted again; it wasn't only weird, it was extremely uncomfortable. And she was almost flat-chested, too!

The irrelevant thought restored Thack's humor. He realized that Barbara's less than abundant measurements really were irrelevant. It was the woman he found fascinating, not the packaging.

Umm, this turn of events calls for investigation, Thack decided. Perhaps he'd amble out to the Holcomb place and offer his assistance to the ladies.

The painkiller was getting to him. His eyelids drooping, Thack settled in for a solid twelve hours of sleep, an anticipatory smile curving his lips.

Barbara woke to a room already made stifling by the relentless rays of the West Texas sun. Her hair, free of the topknot she'd arranged it in the day before, clung in damp tendrils to her perspiration-moist neck. Sliding her hand under the heavy tresses, Barbara lifted the strands away from her skin as she sat up and swung her legs over the edge of the bed.

Hot or not, the undisturbed sleep she'd enjoyed had left her feeling rested and ready to face just about anything the world had to offer, which was surprising, considering that Barbara had not felt completely rested for a very long time.

More acclimatized to the East Coast where long, hot days slide into long, sweltering nights, Barbara had been surprised to find herself reaching for cover during the night to ward off the chill in the air.

Strange country, she mused, tugging her short night-shirt over her head. Maybe a little too strange.

Ten minutes later, Barbara ambled into the kitchen, a scolding protest leaping to her lips at the sight of her aunt, propped awkwardly at the stove.

"Aunt Ellie, what are you doing?"

Barbara hurried across the room. She felt like she was in the midst of an instant replay of a scene she'd been through before. Last night, Barbara had found Ellie in the same position—balanced on crutches while dexter-ously preparing supper. Even handicapped, Ellie had served a delicious meal.

"I'm fixing breakfast, a'course. What does it look like?" Ellie cocked her head sideways and raised her brows.

"But why?" Barbara demanded, sighing in exasper-ation. "I told you last night that I'd prepare the meals from now on."

"And I told you that when the day came that I couldn't get a simple meal together I'd know I was ready for the house with hinges on the roof," Ellie re-torted dryly.

Barbara shivered delicately. The previous evening her aunt's analogy had stumped her. Now she knew that Ellie's reference to a house with hinges on the roof meant a coffin.

"I wish you wouldn't say things like that!" Barbara exclaimed, moving to the cupboard for plates and cups.

"Why not?" Ellie attempted a shrug. "We're all headed there eventually anyway." Her movements were slow but precise as she transferred scrambled eggs and bacon from the frying pan to the plates.

"I know." Barbara had a flashing memory of Thack telling her there was a dead man on the other side of the bluff. "But that doesn't mean we have to discuss it," she went on softly, experiencing an odd sensation of defeat as she assisted Ellie into a chair. "*Especially* over breakfast."

After carrying the food and coffeepot to the table, she seated herself opposite Ellie. "Okay?" she asked hopefully.

"Young people are so touchy about the finality of life," Ellie muttered. "But okay," she agreed with a grin. "Now dig in, you're much too skinny."

Barbara paused in the act of lifting her fork to her mouth. "*I'm* too skinny?" She gave a short burst of laughter. "What about you?" She ran a slow, deliberate gaze over her aunt's gaunt frame.

"My figure don't matter a damn," Ellie shot back. "I'm old."

"You are not old!" Barbara repeated her assertion of the day before. "But I know what you mean. I *feel* old." An unconscious sigh whispered through her soft lips. "And very, very tired."

Ellie's fork clattered to the table. "Barbara Ann Holcomb!" Incredulity colored her tone and widened her faded eyes. "What kind of decadent life-style have you been living in New York City?" she questioned suspiciously.

"Decadent?" Barbara's pleasant laughter sounded in the narrow room. "Oh, Aunt Ellie, that's priceless!" Caught without hankie or tissue, she wiped her amusement-wet eyes with the back of her hand. "Believe me, maintaining a ten- to twelve-hour workday leaves very little time for decadence."

"Well, that's it then." Ellie smiled smugly. "You've been working too hard. It's time you had a long vacation."

"But not too long." Barbara's lips curved ruefully. "I can't afford to be away from the action for any length of time. I can be easily replaced, and I know it. The modeling business is highly competitive."

Ellie's eyes narrowed in speculation. "What you need, young lady, is a husband," she said flatly.

"To take me away from it all?" Barbara managed a tight smile around the sudden thickness in her throat.

"Exactly." Ellie nodded sharply. "And to take care of you."

"I am perfectly capable of taking care of myself." The creamy eggs were suddenly tasteless; Barbara swallowed with difficulty. "I've invested my earnings carefully. If I can hold on in the business for just a few more years, I'll be financially safe." A dry smile shadowed her lips. "Not rich, mind you," she clarified, "I'll still have to do some kind of work.... But then, I enjoy working. But I will have a, well, a cushion, so to speak."

"Nothin' wrong with that." Ellie nodded again. "But a woman needs more than a cushion. She needs a man of her own, and possibly a family."

Barbara's smile disappeared entirely and the thick sensation in her throat increased. She had thought, had dreamed, of a man and family of her own. But she had set her sights on the wrong man. Now older, wiser, more wary, she decided that facing the future on her own was safer and a lot less painful. The problem was explaining her position to her aunt *without* explaining her reasons. Barbara opted for diversionary tactics.

"You managed without husband or family," she pointed out gently.

"You're half right, honey." Ellie's faraway smile was as puzzling to Barbara as her aunt's words. "But only half right. I was never able to have children."

Barbara's confusion deepened. As far as she knew, Ellie had never married. Wasn't her name still Holcomb? Yet, here she was hinting at having had a husband. Several questions rushed into her head at the same time. Before she could voice the first and obvious query, Ellie's head snapped up and her eyes narrowed in concentration.

"Is something wrong?" Barbara jumped out of her chair with alarm. "Are you in pain?"

"Someone's coming," Ellie muttered tersely.

Just as Ellie made the announcement, Barbara heard the rumble of the approaching vehicle as it made its way to the house.

"I wasn't expecting anybody."

Barbara's gaze shot to her aunt's face at the odd, fearful note in her voice. Ellie's entire body seemed to quiver with tension and her expression revealed stark fear. Fear? Barbara frowned. What in the world was Ellie afraid of? Moving to her, Barbara touched Ellie's shoulder gently.

"What is it? What are you afraid of?"

Ellie didn't answer. Groping for her crutches, she waved her hand at the base cabinet beside the sink. "In the top drawer over there you'll find a pistol. Bring it to me."

Barbara's stomach muscles clenched. "A pistol," she repeated hoarsely. Then, in a croak, "A pistol! What do you want with a pistol?"

"Out here a body has to protect themselves," Ellie grunted, wielding the crutches into position under her arms. "And I sent Matt and Zeb out to replace fence posts this morning." Her head whipped around and she leveled a stern look on Barbara. "Move, girl! Bring me that gun."

The bark of Ellie's sharp voice was as effective as a slap; Barbara ran for the cabinet and yanked open the drawer. The gun was small, black, and deadly looking. A shiver of revulsion feathering her shoulders and arms, Barbara forced her hand toward the weapon. Lifting the gun gingerly by the handle, she thrust her arm out straight and carried it back to her aunt.

"Do—" Barbara had to pause to wet her dry lips. "Do you know how to use this thing?" She gratefully relinquished the ugly weapon into her aunt's bony-fingered hand.

"Well a'course I know how to use it." Her words were proven true as she gripped the gun butt firmly. "And I will, too," she added grimly, propelling her body forward with a swing of the crutches, "if I have to."

Confused and oddly frightened, Barbara trailed her aunt to the front door. What *was* going on here? she wondered frantically. Did every person in West Texas answer the door with a gun in their hand? Swallowing back a groan of dismay, she scooted around Ellie to open the door just as a dust-covered pickup truck came to a halt beside the small rented car Barbara had arrived in the day before. Though she couldn't see the man behind the wheel clearly, her aunt's sigh of relief was reassuring.

"Thack." Ellie expelled the name with a pent-up breath. "Open the screen door, honey, so I can get out there." She grinned at Barbara. "Seems like we've got company."

Thoroughly shaken, Barbara complied, then followed Ellie on to the porch, gasping as the hot, dry air closed in around her.

"You'll get used to it, honey," Ellie murmured. Shading her eyes with one awkwardly raised hand, she squinted into the glaring sunlight beyond the shaded porch. "Mornin', Thack. You on official business or just visiting?" she called as Thack carefully exited the truck.

"Mornin' Aunt Ellie, Miz Holcomb." Thack's teeth flashed whitely against his coppery skin. "No official business," he drawled, hobbling toward the porch. "I just stopped by to offer my assistance." His smile widened. "If it's needed."

Even with an injured leg Thack made quick progress to the porch. Watching him silently, Barbara's confusion spread. Only now her uneasy feeling wasn't caused by fright, but by the tingling sensation the sight of the ranger sent skittering through her body.

"Have you had breakfast?" Ellie asked as he mounted the steps to the porch.

"Yes, ma'am," Thack grunted, grimacing as he swung the stiff leg up the last step. "But I sure could do with a cup of your coffee." With a final heaving breath he came to a stop before Ellie.

"I'll get it." Anxious to escape, if only for a moment, Barbara scurried into the house. Then, remembering her aunt's disability, she stopped short. "Can you manage by yourself, Aunt Ellie?'' she asked contritely.

Ellie snorted.

Thack laughed. ''I'll help your aunt, Miz Holcomb, you go on and fix the coffee.'' His laughter deepened at her dubious expression. ''Go on,'' he urged. ''Haven't you ever heard of the lame leading the lame?'' he teased.

''Well,'' Barbara hesitated an instant longer. ''If you're sure you'll be all right?'' She directed her question to her aunt.

Now Ellie laughed. ''Honey, should the need arise, Thack and I could likely hold off an invading army.''

''At least for fifteen minutes or so,'' Thack inserted dryly.

Giving up on the two of them, Barbara stormed into the kitchen. These Texans were crazy! she railed, rinsing the blue agate coffeepot. Were all the residents west of the Pecos this laconic in the face of possible danger? she wondered, sliding the pot onto the burner. And what was keeping them, anyway?

Barbara turned to investigate just as her aunt and Thack hobbled their way into the room. The butt of the nasty-looking little gun was now nestled securely in Thack's hand. A shiver skipped along Barbara's spine as she noted how very natural the weapon looked there.

''Ah, would you please put that thing away?'' A sharp nod of her head indicated the pistol.

Thack frowned. ''This 'thing'?'' he repeated in a curious tone. ''This 'thing' is a beauty.'' Raising his arm he hefted the piece to test its balance.

''It's about as beautiful as a snake!'' Her lips twisted with revulsion as she shifted her glance from the gun to his startled face.

"But snakes *are* beautiful." Thack scowled.

"Yuk!" Barbara shuddered. "Would you please just put it away?" Turning, she gave her full attention to the now perking coffee.

Amazingly, even with his stiff-legged gait, Barbara did not hear Thack come up behind her. However, she knew he was there. The short hairs at her nape acted as an early warning system.

"It's perfectly harmless," Thack confided in a murmur as he slid the gun into the drawer.

Barbara stiffened; she wasn't certain if her reaction was due to his statement or his nearness. "I've heard the propaganda, Mr. Sharp!" Barbara spun around and immediately wished she hadn't. He was so close she could detect the mingled scents of dry West Texas air, healthy human sweat and spicy after-shave on his skin. Swallowing was not easy. "Guns do not kill people, people kill people." She arched one auburn eyebrow disdainfully. "Right?"

A teasing smile twitched his lips, sending her nerves into fits. "Right . . . *Barb*." He accented his deliberate use of the abbreviation of her name. "People kill people."

"But . . ." Barbara paused. Breathing had become as difficult as swallowing. As tall as she was, she had to crane her neck to meet his eyes, some eight inches above her own. And, oh, his eyes! Dark brown and endlessly deep, his eyes held hers in helpless captivity.

"Some people do it fast and clean, others slow and deliberate." His voice had dropped so low that Barbara had to strain to hear it; she was also straining to convince herself of the meaning behind his words. "There are all kinds of ways." A glow lighted his eyes from the inside. "All sorts of methods." As if she knew, instinctively, what was coming, she began to tremble. "I know exactly what ways and methods I'd use with you."

Barbara was no longer aware of her aunt, watching silently from the kitchen table, or the coffeepot, perking merrily away on the stove behind her. She wasn't even aware of the shallow, uneven rasp of her own breath. But she was fully aware of the message woven into Thack's words.

"The death might be brief, Barb," he whispered roughly. "But it would be shatteringly satisfying."

Barbara's breathing ceased entirely. There was a drumming in her ears, as if a large herd of cattle had suddenly started stampeding. Her body ached in a way she had not known for three long years. The heady combination of her imagination and his sensual aura scared her silly. But what scared her the most, and enabled her to break the tension simmering between them, was the certainty that he could deliver on his promise.

The rich aroma rising from the steam from the agate pot wafted to her nostrils and penetrated through her bemusement.

"The—the coffee!" Tearing her gaze from his, she turned slowly, very careful not to make any physical contact with him. "If—" she cleared her parched throat. "If you'll get yourself a cup from the cabinet above the sink—" she closed her eyes in despair at the sound of her breathy voice "—I'll bring the pot to the table."

Thack's only response was a low chuckle.

Flipping the gas jet off, Barbara stared sightlessly at the now madly perking pot. What had happened to her? she cried mutely. What *was* happening to her? It had been years since she'd felt the blood rush with such wild abandon through her veins. And Thack hadn't so much as touched her!

Shaken, Barbara drew a deep breath, attempting to regain her poise. Could it be the air in West Texas that made everybody, including visitors, crazy and reckless? she wondered hopefully.

"Babs, honey, will you bring that leftover cake with the coffee?" Ellie's tone was laced with indulgence.

Barbara's body jerked as if she'd been touched by a live wire and her thoughts scattered in a million directions. Reacting to her aunt's request, she grasped a pot holder and the pot handle with one hand and scooped up the cake plate with the other. Composing her features, she carried the refreshments to the table. She very nearly dropped both pot and cake on sight of the faint yet disturbingly sexy smile that curved Thacks's sensuous male lips.

"Here, I'll take that." Still standing by the table, Thack reached out to relieve Barbara of her burden. The cake plate was whisked from her hand, then his fingers curled around hers on the handle of the coffeepot.

Warmth spread from Barbara's fingertips to her shoulders, then permeated her entire body. This *is* crazy! she thought wildly, relinquishing her hold. Sliding her fingers from under his, which, she noted, were sprinkled with short gold hairs, she sat on the nearest chair.

Thack filled the three cups with the dark brew before carefully lowering his long body onto the chair beside Barbara's. With a muttered grunt, he stretched his injured leg out beneath the table, then favored his companions with a grin.

"Damn thing still hurts." Mild amazement colored his tone.

"What did you expect?" Ellie snorted. "You've been wounded before. You *know* it doesn't magically go away overnight."

A feeling of sickness crawled through Barbara's stomach. Her aunt's words revolved inside her mind. *You've been wounded before.* Barbara could remember seeing the red stain spreading over Thack's thigh. Clutching at her cup, she gulped at the hot liquid and promptly scalded her tongue. Fighting against the rush of tears to her eyes, she gave her reluctant attention to Thack's laconic response.

"Yeah, I know." Raising his cup, he sipped tentatively at the hot brew.

The sensation of sickness intensified inside Barbara. "You—you've been shot before?" she squeaked, eyes wide with horror.

Thack nodded negligently. "Once." Sudden amusement brightened his eyes. "In the same damn leg, come to think of it."

Oh, God! Barbara just managed to keep from blurting the exclamation aloud.

"And that's not counting all the other injuries you've accumulated over the years," Ellie inserted wryly, switching her gaze to Barbara. "I swear, this man's hide must be as tough as saddle leather."

"Other injuries?" Barbara asked weakly, not sure she really wanted to hear.

"Plenty." Grinning, Ellie nodded. "There was a beaut inflicted by a very mean stallion. Remember, Thack?"

"Umm," Thack murmured around the rim of his cup. "How could I forget? Laid me up for two weeks."

"Then there was the time you backed off the roof while helping to repair old man Clayton's shed." Ellie laughed, earning a look of reproof from her niece.

"That was not too bright," Thack ruefully agreed.

Ellie's laughter rang out again. "I could go on and on but—"

"But I think Barbara gets the picture," Thack cut in, his tone one of utter boredom.

Oh, yes, Barbara certainly did get the picture—the man appeared to be a walking disaster! Although she advised herself against commenting, the question slipped out involuntarily.

"You backed off a roof?"

Thack shrugged his unconcern. "Yes, but I wasn't badly hurt; just some bruises and a sprained ankle. It was not a tall structure."

"Falling off the roof didn't leave any lasting scars, but the barbed wire did the time you tangled with that fence," Ellie observed wryly.

Barbed wire? The sickness in Barbara's stomach crawled into her throat. Thack had scarred that beautiful copper-colored hide with barbed wire? Automatically her gaze swept over the areas of exposed skin on his body. The strong column of his throat and the top of his chest were without mark. Her gaze skimmed to his arms, which were visible below the short sleeves of his lightweight shirt. Other than one faint scar on his right forearm, his skin was unmarred.

Though Barbara was aware of the sense of relief shivering through her, she refused to acknowledge it. Where were the scars? she wondered bleakly. She actually jumped when Thack answered her unspoken thought.

"They're on my back," he murmured as he casually refilled his cup. "I was crawling under a fence at the time."

Raising his cup to his lips, Thack blew gently on the still steaming brew. His eyes hooded by narrowed lids, he watched the expressions washing across Barbara's lovely face. The spasms were brief, and difficult to read, but one thing was certain in his mind. Barbara was more than shocked by the idea of the injuries he'd sustained; she was noticeably appalled.

How interesting.

An uneasy silence settled like a dark cloud over the table. Taking advantage of the quiet, Thack sipped at his coffee and studied Barbara over the rim of the cup.

The hip, with-it New York model. Thack hid a smile with a long swallow of coffee. Her face had seemed familiar when they'd met the day before. The puzzle of why he'd felt that flash of recognition had teased him until that morning. She had told him that she modeled in New York, but at the time he'd been somewhat distracted by the wound in his leg. The next morning, while he was devouring his breakfast, he finally realized why it seemed like he knew her. He had seen, and admired, her face on a magazine cover a few months back when he'd been cooling his heels in his dentist's office. At that time, the magazine had been six months old.

And now the hip, with-it model didn't look hip or with-it at all; Barbara Holcomb looked somewhat like she'd swallowed a many-legged creepy crawler.

Ah, yes. Very interesting indeed. Thack concealed a smile by tilting his cup up to drain the contents. Could it be at all possible that the big-city girl felt an attraction for the wild country ranger? he mused, resting his gaze on the enticing curve of her soft lips.

Merely looking at Barbara's mouth made Thack's lips burn with the desire to taste her. The excitement that seared through the lower half of his body had him shifting uncomfortably on the wood chair.

Damn! He wanted her—badly, urgently. He wanted her so badly that had it not been for Ellie, he'd be tempted to take her—here, now.

Beginning to tremble with a need unlike anything he'd ever experienced before, and shocked by its intensity, Thack clamped his back teeth together to exert control over his extraordinary response. A shiver of relief chilled his spine when Ellie broke the prolonged silence—and his flight of erotic fancy.

"Er—you're sure you're not on any official business, Thack?"

Thack frowned at the note of strain in Ellie's voice, and at how her tone aroused all of his lawman's instincts.

"No official business, ma'am." Though Thack's tone remained even, his gaze had sharpened. "As a matter of fact, I'm on extended leave of absence."

Ellie's heaving sigh added to the growing suspicion in Thack's mind; something or somebody had set Ellie's nerves to working overtime. The conclusion made, Thack decided to find out what was bothering his friend. Before he could ask, Ellie forestalled him with another question.

"Babs said you had to kill a man yesterday. Anybody I'd know?"

"I doubt it." Thack shrugged. "And *Babs* is only half right." So, her aunt calls her Babs, he mused, watching her brownish-auburn eyebrows draw together in confusion. Personally, *he* preferred Barb.

"Only *half* right?" Barbara repeated quizzically. "I don't understand. You told me the man was dead!"

"I *believed* the man was dead," Thack countered. "Hell, for all I know, he is dead. But, when the authorities arrived on the scene to collect the body, it was gone." Thack's smile was laden with self-derision. "Maybe I'd better practice my aim while I'm on leave."

"That's probably a good idea," Ellie observed seriously. "Especially if the man is alive, and now gunning for you."

A burst of fear spread insidiously in Barbara's chest and sparked a vision of Thack, his long, beautiful body sprawled in the dusty earth, his life force seeping into the thirsty ground.

No! The protest screamed inside her head. Good Lord, no! Barbara compressed her lips to contain the cry. Her eyes wide from the horror of the image, she glanced at Thack. He was copper and white-gold, vibrantly alive and—Barbara frowned. Why was he looking at Aunt Ellie so strangely? Her frown turned to amazement when he spoke.

"And who's gunning for *you*, Ellie?"

Four

"Wh—what do you mean?" Ellie's face drained of all color; her eyes widened, revealing the white around the faded blue. "What do you know about it?"

It? Startled by her aunt's violent reaction to Thack's soft query, Barbara stared at Ellie in consternation. It? What *was* her aunt talking about?

It. The single word confirmed Thack's suspicions. Ellie was frightened of someone. A slow, intense anger began building in his mind along with a determination to get the truth out of the woman. What kind of scum would frighten an old lady? he wondered, deliberately fanning the anger into protective fury.

None of the emotions churning in Thack were revealed as he leaned back in the chair with deceptive laziness.

"What do I know about what?" He arched his white-gold brows questioningly.

Ellie shook her head frantically. "Nothing!" Her throat worked with the effort to swallow. "It's nothing!"

"Aunt Ellie!" Confused and concerned, Barbara pushed back her chair to go to her aunt. Thack's hand, clamping onto her shoulder, stopped her. Even in her anxious state, Barbara felt the shock from his touch zing from her shoulder to the pit of her stomach. Slicing a glance at him, she opened her mouth to protest. Thack kept her silent with a sharp shake of his head.

"Come on, Ellie," he crooned, coaxingly. "You know you can trust me. Tell me what's got you so damned rattled."

"I—I—" Her eyes shifted from Thack to Barbara then back again to Thack. "Thack, I didn't break my ankle by falling down. I was knocked down." The admission made, Ellie bit down hard on her lip and clenched her fingers agitatedly.

"Knocked down!" Barbara yelped. "But why—who?"

"Easy, honey," Thack cautioned in that same crooning tone.

Barbara was so upset and outraged she hardly noticed his casual endearment. "But Thack—" she began, only to have him cut her off.

"We'll get to the bottom of this." He flashed Barbara a reassuring smile before returning his attention to her aunt. "Won't we, Ellie?" he insisted gently.

"Thack, you don't understand!" Ellie moaned. "I'm so afraid."

Thack's beautifully male features softened with tenderness, surprising Barbara and comforting Ellie. "I can see that you're afraid. So, make me understand why," he cajoled.

Ellie's eyes shifted between them again. "It's a long story," she muttered.

A smile curving his lips, Thack settled into the chair. "I have all the time in the world," he reminded her quietly. "I'm on leave—remember?"

"Yes, I remember, but . . ." Ellie's voice trailed away on an uncertain note.

The tension humming through Barbara broke what little control she'd managed to hang on to. "Aunt Ellie, please tell us!" she pleaded. "Why are you so frightened?"

Ellie held out a moment longer, then her resolve crumbled. "I had some gold," she blurted. "They stole it!"

Without moving as much as a hair, Thack appeared to snap to attention. "Gold?" he queried softly. "They?" His gaze slid to Barbara, who lifted her shoulders helplessly, then back to the older woman. "Maybe you'd better start at the beginning."

Ellie slumped back in the chair. "The gold was here all the time. I never knew about it. Frank told me where it was right before he died," she recited in a monotone.

"Where did Frank get the gold?"

"Who's Frank?"

Barbara and Thack spoke simultaneously. Her eyes cloudy with sadness, Ellie gazed across the table at Barbara.

"Frank *was* my common-law husband." A ghost of a smile moved over her thin lips at the expression of incredulity that widened Barbara's eyes. "He died of a heart attack six weeks ago."

"Common law," Barbara echoed softly. In her mind she heard Thack's comment of the previous afternoon when she had told him of her aunt's injury. *And old Frank not there to help her.*

"Yes, common law." Ellie sighed. "We were together for almost thirty years."

"Thirty years!" Barbara exclaimed, astounded that her aunt had been with a man for more years than she herself had been on the earth and she'd never even known about it. "But—but why didn't you get married?" she blurted artlessly.

"Mind your own business, Barb," Thack ordered in a much too even tone.

Sudden anger flashed in the hazel eyes Barbara sliced to Thack. Who did this accident-prone ranger think he was? she fumed. "Ellie is my only living relative," she snapped. "Her business is my business." Her voice lowered warningly. "And don't call me Barb."

"Okay," Thack agreed readily, a taunting smile lifting the corners of his mouth. "I'll call you honey."

Barbara's nostrils flared with her sharply indrawn breath. "You...you'll do nothing of the—" she began furiously, inwardly fighting an unnerving leap of excitement.

"Do you two want to hear this story?" Renewed strength, and wry amusement, laced Ellie's tone. "Or would you rather I left the room so you can fight?" Her faded eyes twinkled as she glanced from Barbara to Thack. "Or, better yet, make love?"

"Aunt Ellie!" Barbara screeched.

"That's a terrific idea!" Thack grinned wickedly, then sighed heavily. "But I suppose we'd better hear your story."

Struggling with a confusing mixture of anger and sensual awareness, Barbara clamped her trembling lips together and glared at the infuriating man seated lazily beside her.

Obviously fighting the laughter twitching his lips, Thack pursed his mouth in a semblance of a kiss for Barbara before returning his attention to Ellie.

"She's sulking," he told the older woman conversationally. "If we're lucky, she'll pout till you've finished your story."

Ellie lost the battle against a chuckle.

Barbara wished she could breathe fire at Thack. Nothing, she vowed, absolutely nothing, would compel her to speak until after her aunt had completed her narrative! Sulking indeed.

Ellie's chuckle smoothed to a soft smile as she gazed at her niece's mutinous expression. "Oh, Babs, honey, don't be mad at your old aunt. You're all I have left in the world."

Tilting his head, Thack coolly watched Barbara. Though he didn't utter a word, she had the distinct impression that he was telling her to lighten up. She held out a moment, then her tight lips eased into a smile.

"I'm sorry, Aunt Ellie." Reaching across the width of the table, she grasped her aunt's hands with her own. "Please, continue with your story." Out of the corner of her eye, Barbara saw Thack's forbidding expression melt.

"Good girl," he murmured. Turning back to Ellie, he urged, "In your own way, Ellie."

The older woman straightened abruptly and folded her hands on the tabletop. "Well, first off, Barbara, I never married Frank because he was already married and his wife refused to consider a divorce." The obvious question sprang into Barbara's mind; Ellie answered it before she could put it into words. "Frank loved me; I know that for a fact. But he respected his wife's position. She's Mexican-American, and a devout Catholic." Ellie lifted her shoulders fatalistically. "So, I had to respect her position or lose him. And I loved the old codger, honey. More than my own life."

Her aunt's admission, so simply stated, brought sympathetic tears to Barbara's eyes. At another time, she'd examine the rush of emotion that she was experiencing—feelings of admiration and compassion for her aunt mixed, oddly, with a sense of her own inadequacy. But that would have to wait. For now, Barbara nodded her head in understanding, and smiled encouragingly.

"Frank knew he was going to die," Ellie continued steadily. "The night before that final attack took him from me, he told me about the gold. It was stolen."

"What?" Barbara breathed disbelievingly.

"When?" Thack demanded shrewdly.

"A long time ago," Ellie responded to Thack. "During the California gold-rush days. The gold was valued at over thirty-thousand dollars when it was stolen. I suspect it's worth a lot more today."

"I suspect you're right," Thack inserted dryly. "What form is it in—dust? Nuggets?"

Ellie shook her head. "It was stolen as nuggets, but as it was passed from generation to generation, someone had it smelted and fashioned into bullion bars."

"Good night, Nurse!" Thack exclaimed in an awed tone.

"Yeah," Ellie concurred. "My sentiments exactly."

Barbara's eyebrows came together in consternation. "But then, how did your Frank come by the gold? I mean, it's obvious that he didn't steal it."

"The same way I came by it, honey," Ellie explained. "It was handed to Frank by a great-uncle who was on his death bed at the time." She shrugged. "The uncle told Frank that the gold was originally stolen by Frank's great-grandfather's brother."

"So why didn't you report the attack and robbery to the proper authorities?" Thack frowned.

Ellie tossed him a startled look. "Thack! I just told you that the gold was stolen!" She shook her head. "I was afraid to report it."

"Afraid of what?" Barbara and Thack spoke as one.

"Afraid they'd charge me with possession of stolen goods, that's what!"

"Oh, Ellie," Thack said chidingly. "Surely you've heard of the statute of limitations? The crime is a hundred years old and probably wouldn't be listed in police records. The gold is yours," he sighed, "or at least it was. Tell me exactly what happened, and when."

"Mine!" Ellie looked about ready to explode. "You mean I owned it? Legally?"

"I don't know why not." Thack's shoulders moved in another brief shrug. "You may have to register an amount of that size, but other than that, I would say the gold is definitely yours—" he grimaced "—or *was* yours. When *did* all this happen, Ellie?"

"Two weeks ago yesterday." Ellie's tone had regained full strength and was now laced with outraged anger. "I thought they had come to offer me condolences, but the sneaky bastards knocked me flat and tore the place apart till they found the gold!"

"Come to offer you condolences?" Thack repeated softly. Then his eyes narrowing, "You knew these men, Ellie?"

"Yeah—well, not really." Ellie sighed. "I don't know their names or anything, but I'd seen them a couple of times before. They'd talk to Frank when we'd go into town for supplies."

"Can you identify them?" Thack insisted sharply.

Though Ellie looked startled, she answered at once. "Yes, a'course I can identify them. Why?"

Instead of answering, Thack shot another question at her. "Could they have thought you were dead?"

"I suppose they could have." Ellie's lips twisted. "I hit my head when I went down, and I sure was dead to the world for a while. Why?" she repeated.

Having latched onto Thack's train of thought almost immediately, Barbara replied for him. "Because once they figure out that you're not dead, Aunt Ellie, they'll be back. It's not safe here."

"Bull's-eye," Thack grunted. "I think it would be best for you to move into town for a while, Ellie."

"I'll do nothing of the kind!" Ellie retorted indignantly. "Move into town indeed." She gave an unladylike snort. "I'm not leaving my home, and that's final."

"Then I think you'll have two houseguests for a while," Thack observed mildly. "*I* will not leave you two women here unprotected." He smiled as both aunt and niece opened their mouths to protest, and continued before either could speak, "And *that's* final."

The narrow room was once again shrouded in an uneasy silence as the two women thought over his ultimatum.

Up until that point, Barbara had taken little notice of the increasing heat as the temperature inched its way toward a hundred degrees. Now, suddenly, the heat seemed stifling. Beginning to perspire, she squirmed in the hard chair.

Darn it! She didn't want Thack's company; she didn't want to be anywhere near him! Barbara fumed, staring down at her clasped hands. Thack aroused sensations and feelings she had no desire to experience. For her peace of mind *and* physical well-being, she silently urged her aunt to send him packing.

Mulling over Thack's flat statement, Ellie glanced across the table at her niece. A smile teased the edges of her lips as she studied Barbara's expressive face.

Well, well, Ellie mused, what have we here? Why should the idea of Thack being in the house for a few days agitate Babs so? she wondered in knowing amusement. She had been fully aware of the electrical tension flowing between Barbara and Thack from the minute he arrived—hell, a body would have had to be unconscious not to have noticed *their* awareness of each other!

Although she'd been on the verge of giving Thack an argument about his staying at the ranch, Ellie changed her mind as a sly smile formed on her face.

"I do have that gun, and old Matt and Jeb, a'course," she murmured, shifting her gaze from Thack to her niece.

"Then again," Thack drawled, "you did have the gun and old Matt and Jeb when you were attacked the first time," he pointed out. "Didn't you?"

Ellie dredged up a sigh. "Ye-ess—but..." She let her voice trail helplessly away.

Barbara cast a wary glance at Thack; the man looked much too self-satisfied. "Maybe we should move into town for a few weeks, Aunt Ellie," she almost pleaded.

"Out of the question," Ellie replied promptly. "I'm not about to let three half-baked thieves chase me away from *my* home."

Barbara slumped against the back of her chair in defeat.

Thack straightened in his chair alertly. "Okay, it's settled, I'll stay here. Now, Ellie, I'd like you to describe your assailants to me."

Her face set into lines of concentration, Ellie endeavored to describe her attackers to Thack. She was detailing the third and final assailant when Thack sat forward, his expression hardening.

"That son of a bitch," he muttered when Ellie had finished.

"You know one of them?" Barbara inquired, ignoring his expletive.

Pushing himself to his feet, Thack made a hobbling circuit of the table before coming to a halt next to Barbara's chair. "Yeah," he replied after a long pause. "The third man Ellie described is none other than my missing dead cattle rustler." He raked his hand through his hair, tousling the neatly brushed curls. "Now I'm positive I'm not leaving you two alone out here."

Barbara couldn't control the reflexive movement of her eyes as her glance shot to the kitchen's single window, as if afraid a face was peering in at them. "Then that means at least one of the thieves is still in the area," she murmured shakily, dragging her gaze back to Thack.

"It also means that they haven't unloaded the gold yet," he observed thoughtfully.

Ellie bolted upright in her chair. "How do you figure that?" she voiced the question that had also occurred to Barbara.

"Com'on, Ellie," Thack sent the older woman a chiding grin. "I was chasing the jerk yesterday for rustling cattle the night before. Why would a man with a third of over thirty-thousand dollars in his poke be out risking his hide stealing beef?"

"Yes, you're right!" Barbara exclaimed in excitement. "That must mean that they still have Aunt Ellie's gold!"

"Beef." Thack grinned, unpleasantly. "It could also mean that they're holed up somewhere and running out of supplies." He nodded, as if certain in his own mind. "And if they're snatching cattle outside Sanderson, they're probably not too far away."

Ellie frowned in confusion. "But it's been two weeks. Why wouldn't they have sold the gold by now?"

Barbara looked at Thack expectantly.

"I'd hazard a guess that they haven't been able to find someone to take the 'hot' metal off their hands." His grin widened. "If you'll excuse the pun."

Ellie laughed.

Barbara groaned and muttered: "A very bad pun."

Thack continued. "They're obviously amateurs and very likely approaching small-time fences who wouldn't have the resources to buy the gold." His head dipped sharply; he was certain that his gut instincts were right. "Oh, yeah. They're still in the Pecos, and they still have the gold." He turned to level a riveting stare on Ellie. "You'd better notify the authorities."

Her back ramrod straight, Ellie returned his stare, and issued a challenge. "I'll split the gold fifty-fifty with you if you track the thieves down and get it back for me."

Thack looked momentarily stunned. "But I don't want your gold, Ellie!" he protested. "Besides, I'm wounded—remember?"

"So's one of the thieves," she reminded him.

"But there are three of them," Thack tacked on.

"Which makes it about even, I'd say," Ellie countered complacently.

Barbara's head had swiveled back and forth between them. Now her gaze fastened on her aunt. "Why not notify the authorities and let them handle it?" she asked in bemusement, while silently wondering if Thack was really the equal to three potentially dangerous men.

"My question exactly," Thack agreed, returning to his chair and slowly lowering his long body onto it.

"Oh, Thack," Ellie sighed. "You know all the rigmarole attached to a routine police investigation. All the questions and red tape, along with the gossip and rumors. I don't want every blessed soul between here, El Paso, and all the way to San Antonio to know that I had that gold."

"Yes, I can understand that but—" Thack began.

"Thack, please," Ellie interrupted. "You could find the men *and* my gold, and then give all the particulars to the authorities." Her tone tugged at the heartstrings, entreating her listeners to take pity on her plight. But then her tactics changed. "Please, you go out and find those low-life varmints who knocked me down and stole my retirement fund."

Barbara felt like she was reading her aunt's letter again; Ellie could manipulate along with the pros! A quick glance at Thack's wryly amused expression told her he was wise to her aunt's cajolery. Even so, Thack capitulated.

"Okay, Ellie, I'll see what I can find out." He held up one hand as a delighted smile spread over the old lady's face. "Don't start thanking me yet. I only said I'd nose around a little. I'm not making any promises."

"I didn't ask for promises," Ellie reminded him. "Only some help. And you *will* help?" she persisted.

Thack sighed, but smiled good-naturedly. "Yes, Ellie, I'll help. If I can." Once again he heaved his elongated frame from the chair. "And I suppose I might as well get at it." He cocked an eyebrow at her. "The phone's in the living room—right?"

Ellie nodded. "On my desk, by the window."

Barbara was besieged by a multitude of conflicting emotions as she watched Thack hobble from the room. The scrape-thud of his heels drew her gaze to his scuffed boots, then up, following the length of his long, muscular legs to his slender, tight buttocks and narrow waist encircled by a wide leather belt. From his waist up, his torso appeared as an upside-down triangle, widening at his muscle-corded back to the breadth of his shoulders.

Was Thack's body that same burnished gold color all over? In Barbara's mind, his faded jeans and sandtoned shirt dissolved, revealing taut gold skin, stretched over long bones and hard muscles.

The flashing image wrenched a sigh of longing from her chest, and alerted her to the strongest of the emotions battling inside. Every nerve in her body was clamoring for him!

Shaken, Barbara stared breathlessly at the empty doorway. She wanted Thack urgently—more than she'd ever wanted anything before in her life! And she barely knew the man!

"I suppose we'd best get these breakfast dishes cleaned up." Ellie's observation startled Barbara out of her sensuous bemusement.

"What?"

Ellie smiled, knowingly, understandingly. "He is some kind of man, isn't he, honey?"

"Yes," Barbara whispered, rattled beyond subterfuge. "He scares the hell out of me."

Ellie blinked, then laughed uncertainly. "But why?" She frowned, looking confused. "Thack's a fine man. In what way does he scare you?"

In the most basic way. Barbara kept her immediate response to herself. "Oh, he's—he's—" she raked her mind for words to justify her blurted confession. She finally grasped at his seemingly detached manner. "He's so tough!" Jumping to her feet, she began clearing the table. "I mean, Thack actually believed he'd killed that thief, and it didn't faze him in the least." Turning away, she carried the dishes to the sink. "I simply don't understand a man like that."

"What's to understand? The man was doing his job."

Barbara went absolutely still, her hand clasping the plastic bottle of dish detergent. Her aunt hadn't replied; instead the response had come from the man under discussion. A tinge of pink spread from her throat to her cheeks and the heat she felt could not be blamed on the temperature outside. It was obvious he'd overheard her.

"No scathingly witty comeback?" Thack taunted when she failed to reply. "Perhaps it would have been more acceptable to you if I'd kept my weapon holstered and allowed that scum to gun me down." There was a steely quality to his tone that Barbara hadn't heard before.

"Thack!" Ellie protested. Whether she was reacting to his remark or his tone, Barbara had no way of knowing.

The thoughts she'd experienced earlier rose to torment her. The vision of Thack being gunned down caused a shudder to shake her slight frame. Her reaction was the same as before. Dear God, no! She opened her mouth to voice the denial just as his tone slashed at her with the force of a whip.

"Look at me, damn you!" he ordered sharply.

Stung, Barbara whirled around, and found herself confronting a stranger—a very hard-faced stranger.

"Thack, please!" The protest again came from Ellie, who was struggling to her feet.

Thack's gaze remained riveted to Barbara's shocked eyes. "I won't hurt her, Ellie," he promised in a gentler tone. "But I think it might be time for Miss Holcomb to grow up and face a few facts of life."

"I am fully aware of the facts of life, Mr. Sharp!" Barbara retaliated, drawing herself up to her full five feet nine inches. Almost instinctively, her hand hefted the detergent bottle.

"You lob that thing at me and you're in big trouble, honey." A hint of laughter was woven through Thack's warning tone.

Startled, Barbara gazed at the bottle in her hand. Had she actually been about to fling it at him? she wondered in amazement. She had never resorted to force before—never!

"Ah—umm, if you will excuse me?" Ellie's voice held a note of sheer glee. "I think the phone's about to ring." Chuckling softly, she swung the crutches, and her body, out of the kitchen.

Ellie's chuckle was echoed in Thack's deep tones.

"Would you have chucked it?" A nod of his head indicated the bottle in Barbara's hand as he crossed the room to her.

"I—I don't know," she admitted. "But I was tempted." As he approached, Barbara pressed back against the hard sink. What was that saying about a rock and a hard place? she thought, excitement leaping through her body.

"I'd have retaliated, you know." Thack was so close that Barbara could feel his warm breath caress her cheeks.

"You—you'd have, ah, thrown it back?" Oh, why wouldn't her tongue work properly? Barbara felt a surge of despair over the breathiness of her response to his question.

A smile that was devilishly sexy teased the corners of his lips. "I was thinking more along the lines of throwing *you* back." His voice reflected his sexy smile. "Onto the floor—and under me." He lowered his head with slow deliberation.

Her breathing grew shallow, erratic, and her resistance began to evaporate as Barbara unconsciously parted her lips in anticipation of his kiss.

"Aware of the facts of life, are you? I'll be the judge of that." His murmur reached her ears an instant before his lips touched hers.

Thack's kiss was gentle and sizzlingly electric. Barbara's bones seemed to evaporate along with the last of her resistance. As a choking moan filled her throat, she dropped the plastic bottle from nerveless fingers and curled her arms around his taut neck.

She felt a groan against her mouth, then Thack pulled her into his arms, crushing her breasts against his hard chest and her lips with his own.

Sensation after wild sensation rippled up through Barbara's trembling body, exploding into a million fragments that pierced her senses with urgent messages. Responding to her tremors, Thack stroked the sensitive skin on the inside of her bottom lip with the tip of his tongue while slowly sliding his fingers down her spine to its tingling base.

Barbara didn't think, she reacted. Shuddering from an intensity she'd never experienced, not even with Peter, she arched her body into the hard arousal of his and returned his kiss with greedy hunger.

Her aggressiveness was met with another, deeper growl and the driving thrust of Thack's warm tongue. Barbara met him halfway by parting her lips wider to allow him free access to her mouth.

Accepting her silent invitation, Thack deepened the kiss, and clasped her curving bottom with his broad hands to pull her tightly to him.

What *was* she doing? How could she let him . . . The feeble protest from her conscience was stilled by the hard pressure of his blatant masculinity. Responding to the most basic of instincts, her body curved softly, pliantly into his.

The kiss was finally ended, and drawing ragged breaths, Thack's mouth sought the satiny curve of Barbara's arched throat. "I was wrong," he muttered roughly, gliding his tongue to the wildly beating pulse in her throat. "You do know the facts of life."

He slid his hands up and under the cotton crop top she'd pulled on that morning. As his tongue touched the hollow at the base of her throat, his hands took possession of her small, aching breasts while his fingers tested the gem-hard crests. "And you definitely are grown up."

Raising his head, Thack slowly ran his gaze over her flushed cheeks and kiss-reddened lips. Then, as his hands drew the shirt up and away from her body, his gaze drifted down to her small pointed breasts.

"You might not be quite as grown up as the other women I've known—" his broad chest rose and fell with his sharply indrawn breath "—but, damned if you're not the sexiest!"

The mention of the "other" women he had known sent a chill through Barbara that froze the molten heat at her core. She required no definition of his use of the word *known*. She knew full well what he'd meant. For some inexplicable reason the very idea of Thack, physically *knowing* another woman, any other woman, cut her to the quick like a jagged-edged blade.

"What is it? What's wrong?" Though she hadn't moved, Thack obviously sensed her withdrawal. "What did I say to upset you?"

Feeling unable to speak, Barbara shook her head and raised her hands to press against his chest. Though he frowned his displeasure as her shirt dropped down, Thack obligingly stepped back, away from her. Without uttering a word, Barbara skirted around him and dashed for the doorway.

"Barb!" Thack called after her. "Where are you going?"

Barbara didn't answer, she couldn't. Her breaths sounding like sharp little sobs, she slipped into her room and shut the door. Leaning back against the rough panels, she closed her eyes. Where was she going? Before she could answer his question, she had to answer her own.

Five

———

What was she doing?

Slumped against the door, Barbara drew deep breaths and silently repeated the question. The query had nothing to do with her escape from Thack, and she knew it. The question concerned her own loss of physical and emotional control.

Pushing her perspiring body away from the wooden support, she walked to the bed and dropped onto it.

What had come over her? Flinging an arm up over her head, Barbara stared sightlessly at the open-beamed ceiling. Thackery Sharp was a virtual stranger to her, yet she had not only allowed him to kiss her, but she'd permitted him to intimately caress her. And she had returned that intimacy with equal fervor!

It had been more than three years since Barbara had been stirred to a blaze by a man's touch. And even Peter had never possessed the power to create such an all-encompassing flame.

The mere thought of the fire Thack had ignited in her caused a shiver to dance along Barbara's spine. Lord, she had wanted him—still wanted him!

Beginning to ache all over again, Barbara slid her tongue along her bottom lip, imagining that she could taste him on her mouth, feel him *in* her mouth.

And Thack would be staying at the ranch, would sleep in the house every night! Barbara was neither naive nor stupid. She realized the attraction between them would intensify with proximity. The situation was potentially combustible. A mixture of anticipation and dread shuddered through her body. How many nights would pass before she found Thack in her bed, or herself in his? she asked herself.

Her imagination conjured up the scene, and Barbara could envision Thack's long, golden-bronze body stretched out on the bed beside her.

The sound of her low moan lay heavily on the hot air in the small room, and propelled Barbara off the bed. Shivering as if she were freezing in the ninety-odd degrees, she stood beside the bed, her head moving slowly back and forth in silent denial.

Had she walked away from one handsome user only to succumb to another? Though the one was dark and broodingly intense, and the other glitteringly golden and charmingly laid-back, in Barbara's sight Peter and Thack were brothers under the skin. Brothers who pursued the pleasure of the senses while adroitly avoiding any and all emotional commitment.

The values that had been instilled in Barbara by her unyielding New England parents were still strong. She would not go through the devastation of a "no strings" love affair again. She could not. Attraction or not, proximity or not, she would keep Thack at arm's length—one way or another.

Despite the determined set of her chin, Barbara's entire body jerked with fright at the sound of knuckles rapped against the bedroom door. Instinctively she knew those knuckles were part of a broad male hand.

"Yes?" Though low, her voice was steady.

"Your aunt asked me to tell you that lunch is ready." Thack's voice was also low, and edged with impatience.

Barbara swallowed. "Thank you." She sighed at the husky sound of her voice. "Tell her I'll be out in a moment."

"Barb? Are you all right?" Thack's impatience had given way to concern. "You're not crying—are you?"

"No, Thack, I'm not crying." Barbara could summon little more than a whisper.

"Barbara?"

Feeling her resolve weaken at his concern, Barbara stiffened her spine.

"I'll be out in a minute, Thack." Holding her breath, she prayed he'd hear the harsh tone of dismissal in her voice.

By midafternoon the tension inside the ranch house was more intense than the heat outside.

Resting uncomfortably in the straight-backed chair at Ellie's desk, Thack eased his stiffened leg under the small desk and reached for the phone.

As he waited for a response at the other end of the line, a flash of color caught Thack's attention and drew his gaze to the window. As he watched, his heartbeat accelerated.

Barbara was strolling across the uneven dusty yard toward the corral, her face shaded by a wide-brimmed straw hat and oversized sunglasses. Her long, smooth dancer's legs were exposed from the fringes of her cut-off jeans and, as she walked, her slender midriff was visible below the hem of her bright yellow crop top.

Why me? The groan echoed inside his head as Thack closed his eyes to shut out the sight of her. How was a man to concentrate with a distraction like *her* around?

"Hello! Who the hell is it?"

Thack snapped to attention at the irritated sound of the voice at the other end of the line. It had obviously not been the first time the man had answered.

"It's Thack Sharp, Dell." Thack opened one eyelid a crack, winced, then closed it again. "Sorry to keep you waiting. I was...ah, lost in thought." Excitingly erotic thought, he tacked on silently.

"That's okay, Thack. For a minute there, I thought it was some smart ass."

Change the smart to stupid and you'd be close to right. Thack kept that observation to himself as well.

By the time Thack replaced the receiver, a satisfied smile had turned up the corners of his tightened lips. Things were moving along much better than he'd expected. All that was left to be done was to inform the ladies of his plans.

The ladies. Barbara. Thack expelled a long, yearning breath. Damn! And he'd had such hopes for the nights he'd be spending here at the ranch. Now all those hopes went right down the ol' porcelain receptacle. Why me?

The atmosphere around the supper table was every bit as strained as it had been throughout the day. Barely picking at the food on her plate, Barbara replayed the afternoon in her mind.

Not that there was all that much *to* replay! After a tense and mostly silent lunch, during which Ellie had eyed her and Thack warily, Thack had muttered something about having some calls to make and hobbled back to the phone in the living room.

"What's going on between you two?" Ellie had demanded the instant Thack was beyond hearing her lowered voice.

Though Barbara had felt her skin heat with a flush, she'd managed to meet her aunt's stare directly. "Why, nothing's going on. What could be going on?" she'd responded innocently.

Ellie had actually snorted. "Oh, honey, I might be getting old, but I'm not *that* old!"

"I—I haven't the vaguest idea what you're talking about!"

"I'm talking about the way you and Thack look at each other!" Ellie'd retorted. "Why, that man looks at you as though he'd like to gobble you up for dessert!"

"But—"

"And your expression is exactly the same as his," she'd continued, ignoring Barbara's attempt at protest. "Heavens, it'd be obvious to an idiot that you're both itchin' to get your hands on one another."

"Aunt Ellie! Really!" Barbara had gasped.

"Aunt Ellie, really, my foot." Though her tone had been rough, her eyes gleamed with amusement. "Ain't nothin' wrong with two people having a healthy yen for each other. And you and Thack got a yen as big as all outdoors."

"No! I don't—he doesn't!" Shaken by her own transparency, Barbara had been reduced to sputtering. Ellie had merely smiled tolerantly.

"Honey, I'm no fool, and I've known the feeling a time or two. And, Thack—well, Thack's not just a gorgeous hunk o'male animal, he's a fine man. And fine men ain't all that easy to come by. *You'd* be a fool to deny your body's natural instincts."

But deny Barbara did, throughout the afternoon. After the lunch dishes were cleared away and the kitchen restored to order, Ellie had announced her intention of having a nap and she went to her room.

Left to her own devices, Barbara had considered dusting and straightening the living room. She'd rejected the thought almost as soon as it had occurred; Thack was in the room at the desk.

Refusing to think about her aunt's advice, she'd wandered aimlessly around the ranch yard, peering into the barn before settling listlessly on the railed corral.

Earlier, Barbara had briefly met Ellie's hired hands, Matt and Jeb. Both men were in their early sixties, confirmed bachelors, and taciturn to the point of grimness. Nevertheless, when they returned to the house after finishing their chores late that afternoon, Barbara was so sick of her own company, and her exhausting effort *not* to think, that she greeted them like long-lost friends.

Though Matt and Jeb put forth an admirable struggle to answer every one of her admittedly inane questions, it was obvious they thought her more than a trifle stupid.

And they were absolutely correct, Barbara now concluded, jabbing her fork into the tender piece of steak on her plate. Why *was* she getting uptight about Thack?

She had made her decision—hadn't she? Barbara transferred her fork to the refried beans next to the steak. She wasn't interested in gratifying her physical urges for a few nights or a few weeks. She simply did not have the emotional strength to indulge in casual sex—regardless of the current trend or mores.

But, oh Lord, the taste of him was still on her lips!

Barbara was systematically moving the refried beans from one side of the plate to the other when Thack made a statement that halted the pointless action, and jerked her into attention.

"I'll be hitting the trail sometime tomorrow morning."

His casual tone had the impact of a strident shout. For a moment there was absolute silence, then Ellie burst into speech.

"What do you mean, you'll be hitting the trail? I thought you said you would be staying awhile!"

"You asked me to look for your gold—remember?" Thack cocked one white-gold eyebrow at Ellie.

"Well, yes, but—" Ellie shrugged "—you said it wasn't safe here for us." She included Barbara with a sharp nod of her head.

"And I still feel the same," Thack said. "So I've arranged for someone to stay here with you while I'm away."

"Someone?" Ellie repeated, suspiciously. "What someone?"

Thack smiled reassuringly at her. "A friend of mine. His name's Josh Barnet. He's an ex-cop."

"Ex?" Ellie eyed him warily. "The man's retired? How old is he?"

"Not much older than I am, not quite forty." Thack's smile faded. "His retirement was brought about by circumstances, not age.'' Thack's tone hardened. "Four years ago, Josh was involved in a large drug bust that wound up in a wild car chase. The chase ended in a mangled pile-up of several cars. Josh got his man, but lost his left arm in the process.''

Barbara's stomach muscles clenched sickeningly and her mind was numbed with compassion for the unknown man. But, although Ellie's leathery tanned face paled, she didn't lose sight of her position.

"What kind of protection can a one-armed man give us?'' she demanded sharply.

Barbara gasped at her aunt's seeming insensitivity; Thack smiled in understanding.

"One helluva lot more than two ordinary men with two good arms,'' he retorted genially. "Make no mistake, Josh is one tough hombre. He always has been. But he's even more so since he lost his arm and had to retire from the force.'' He grinned wryly. "If I ever find myself in deep sh . . . ah, trouble, the one man I'd want by my side is Josh Barnet.'' His grin broadened. "Fortunately, by my side is very likely where he'd be, seeing as how he works for me.''

Works for him? Barbara frowned. Thack was a Texas Ranger. In what possible capacity could this Josh Barnet work for Thack? Ellie partially answered the question even as it was still forming in Barbara's mind.

"This Josh person works at your ranch?''

Ranch? What ranch? Barbara looked blankly at Thack.

"This Josh person *runs* my ranch,'' he corrected softly.

"I didn't know you had a ranch,'' Barbara inserted.

"There's a lot of things you don't know about me, honey.'' Thack ran a warm molasses gaze from her ankles to her wide hazel eyes. "A lifetime of things. But you will," he promised softly.

The anticipatory tingle that skipped down Barbara's spine propelled her from her chair. Flustered by both his intimate tone and his promise, she tried to hide her reactions by busying herself with clearing the table and changing the topic.

"Where, ah, where is your ranch located?" she asked with forced brightness.

Thack smiled with self-satisfied content. "In the hill country above San Antonio." He supplied the information blandly.

Barbara blinked in surprise. "San Antonio!" she exclaimed. "Not West Texas?" She had begun to think Thack considered West Texas the only place to live.

"Not West Texas," he reaffirmed, laughing quietly. "I'll tell you all about it someday."

The shiver of anticipation intensified along Barbara's spine. Then, the realization hit her that she would very likely be back in New York by the time "someday" rolled around. Squirting detergent into the sink, she applied the dishcloth vigorously to a plate, and refused to acknowledge the disappointment she felt. After all, she really didn't care where or how he lived . . . did she?

Barbara had just about rubbed the pattern of Texas bluebonnets from the plate when the sound of her aunt's voice stopped her.

"So, when's this Josh Barnet person supposed to arrive?" Ellie queried Thack.

Drying her hands on a terry-cloth towel, Barbara turned as Thack responded to Ellie.

"Late tonight or early tomorrow morning." He shrugged. "I'll take off as soon as he's settled in here."

"Take off for where?" The question shot out of Barbara's mouth before she could stop it.

As if her obvious interest in his plans amused him, Thack grinned, revealing strong teeth that flashed whitely in contrast to his golden bronzed skin. Moving lazily, he got to his feet and ambled unevenly to the stove.

"Terlingua," he drawled, grasping the coffeepot and turning back to the table.

"Terlingua ranch?" Ellie frowned.

Thack shook his head negatively as he carefully lowered himself onto the chair again. "The ghost town."

"There's a ghost town?" Barbara was intrigued.

"What for?" Ellie was practical.

"Yes, there's a ghost town," Thack replied to Barbara before shifting his attention to her aunt. "I want to have a look around," he explained. "I picked up some curious information while I was on the phone with one of my contacts this afternoon. Seems like there's been some petty theft of foodstuffs lately in and around Tortilla. It's probably a wild hunch—" his shoulders moved again in a slight shrug "—but I decided to indulge it and go on down to the place and nose around a bit."

"Your hunch being that the gold thieves are holed up in Terlingua?" Ellie asked skeptically.

Thack nodded and sipped at the coffee he'd moments ago poured into his cup. "If not exactly 'holed up' then laying low there and using it as a raiding base."

Forgetting the dishes in the sink, Barbara wandered back to the table. "Raiding base? I don't understand." Hands on her slim hips, she raised her eyebrows at him questioningly.

Thack finished his coffee before answering. "If they haven't been able to sell the gold yet, I figure they just might be out of funds *and* supplies. And, as they'd have no way of knowing that Ellie never reported the theft or gave their descriptions to the authorities, they're probably leery of being recognized if they ventured into a store even if they had the wherewithal to buy supplies." He arched one brow. "Are you with me so far?"

Barbara sighed and gave him an impatient look. "I'm muddling along. Go on."

A muscle jumped in his cheek from his effort to control the smile that twitched his lips. "Ah, yeah." He cleared his throat. "Well, we know that at least one of them has tried a hand at cattle rustling." Absently, Thack massaged his injured thigh. "I'm riding a hunch that they are laying low while trying to get a grubstake together before moving on to greener pastures." He glanced at Ellie. "Make any sense to you?" he asked.

Ellie's eyes narrowed. "Now that you've explained it, yes." She slowly raised her eyelids, revealing a gleam in the faded blue depths. "At first I thought you'd slipped a cog. I mean, who would ever think of rustling gold thieves hiding out at Terlingua? There's nothin' there— exceptin' for once a year when they hold the chili cook-off down there," she qualified.

"Which is exactly why I think they just might have picked that particular spot." Thack grinned. "Hell, even if the odd tourist wandered onto the place, there'd be no reason to suspect a couple of strangers."

Still standing beside the table, Barbara had a faraway look in her eyes. "A ghost town," she murmured, caught up in memories of the Westerns she'd seen during her youth. "How exciting."

"Exciting!" Ellie looked at her niece as if she'd said something hilarious. "Terlingua? Honey, Terlingua's about as exciting as six months without rain."

Barbara felt a flush heat her cheeks. "Well it's exciting to me!" she protested. "I've never seen a ghost town." Tossing her head like a spirited filly, she strolled back to the sink and plunged her hands into the now tepid water. "I not only think it's exciting," she murmured to nobody in particular, "I think it's rather romantic."

"If you can find anything at all romantic in Terlingua," Ellie retorted, "I'd say you really do need a vacation from your job in the big city."

Thack laughed softly, deep in his throat. The sound both pleased and annoyed Barbara. Swinging around to face him she asked sweetly, "Will it be dangerous for you to go there?"

He laughed louder. "Probably not."

Barbara wiped the laughter off his lips with four soft words.

"I'm going with you."

"What?" Thack's face sobered while his spine stiffened.

Barbara smiled, chidingly. "I said: I'm going with you." She enunciated each word distinctly.

"Now wait a minute!" Thack slid his body upright on the hard chair. "I don't know what I'll find there."

Barbara shrugged carelessly. "You just told me it probably wouldn't be dangerous. And I'd love to see a real ghost town."

Thack groaned and glanced appealingly at Ellie. "A romantic!" he muttered. "What would I do with her out there, Ellie?"

"Don't ask me, I only live here," Ellie countered. Then added consideringly, "If you think there'll be no danger, what would be the harm in it, Thack?"

Thack was beginning to look cornered. "But, don't you need her to help you here in the house?" he asked hopefully.

Watching her aunt, Barbara held her breath; for some reason going with Thack was suddenly the most important issue in the world. For all his dismissive attitude, Thack had recently sustained an injury, he was limping and probably weak. She really didn't want to mother-hen him, Barbara assured herself, but she *wanted* to stay close. Avoiding the real reasons for her decision, she stared at her aunt fixedly.

"I managed all right up till yesterday," Ellie snorted, raising Barbara's hopes and sinking Thack's. "You two youngsters just go along and do your investigating. I'll be fine." Sitting back, she smiled with satisfaction. She wasn't matchmaking, she assured herself, she was just sweeping some of the rocks from the road.

Barbara didn't crow. On the contrary, having gained her aunt's support, she began to feel very uncertain of herself and Thack.

"Do you mind, terribly?" she asked Thack, biting down on her lip. "I promise not to bother you," she tacked on appealingly.

Thack caved in, as he knew he would. "Okay, you can come along. But don't complain to me if you're disappointed with the place." Inside his body, anticipation unfurled like a desert flower after a reviving rainfall.

Josh Barnet arrived at the ranch house minutes after Barbara had said good-night to her aunt and Thack.

Curious about the man, she pulled on a lightweight, knee-length robe and returned to the living room.

At first sight, Josh didn't appear at all intimidating or prepossessing. Approximately six feet tall, Josh seemed dwarfed by Thack's six-foot-four frame. Dwarfed and colorless. Whereas Thack was muscular but slender, Josh was whipcord lean and rangy. His hair and skin were dark in contrast to Thack's overall golden bronze appearance. He was dressed in close-fitting jeans, a washed-out blue shirt and scarred boots with worn-down heels. And, from across the width of the room, he appeared to possess two perfectly good, usable arms! His right hand was clasped in Thack's, his left hung by his side and was encased in a black leather glove.

As Thack turned from greeting Josh he caught sight of her, hesitating in the living-room doorway. Drawing the man with him, Thack walked to where Ellie was ensconced in an overstuffed chair, watching the interchange with obvious interest.

"Come meet J.B.," Thack invited, indicating his friend with a slight movement of his head.

Smiling politely, Barbara entered the room. As she came to a halt beside Thack, Josh turned to slide an assessing head-to-toe glance over her. Barbara immediately revised her initial opinion of him. Josh Barnet had the most incredibly deep sapphire-blue eyes she'd ever seen. Clear as the gem they matched in color, his eyes were just as glitteringly cold and hard. Stifling a gasp of shock, Barbara managed to maintain her smile as she extended her hand to him.

While Thack rattled off the introductions, Barbara examined the man's features through lowered lashes. Her visual inventory sent a chill to the pit of her stomach. His facial bones were prominently highlighted under the dark skin stretched tautly over his face. There were hollows beneath his eyes and cheekbones. His jawline had the appearance of having been hacked from rock by a dull chisel. His lips were devoid of any softening fullness. Everything about him underlined Thack's pithy description of him as one "tough hombre."

But, by far, the most shocking thing about Josh Barnet was his voice. Deep, soft, his voice had the soothing texture of rich velvet. On the spot, Barbara decided that Josh's voice alone had very likely melted the hearts of women of all ages.

Bemused and mildly beguiled, Barbara heard only the tenor of his voice, not the actual words he spoke to her. Thack's sudden movement shattered her daze.

"I'm going to get something for J.B. to eat and a beer for both of us." Tilting his head, he leveled a piercing gaze at Barbara, leaving little doubt in her mind that he'd correctly read her reaction to his ranch manager. "Will you ladies join us?" There was a steely quality to his tone that made the invitation a definite command, a command backed up by a challenging smile.

Barbara was under no illusions. Thack knew she was both repelled and fascinated by Josh. She was fully aware that Thack was challenging her to sit across the table and converse with his friend. She accepted his dare by lifting her chin and flashing him a brittle smile.

Ellie, long past the age of indulging in games of any sort, excused herself and retired for the night. Having taken Josh's measure at once, Ellie was neither fascinated nor repelled by the man; she was simply assured of his ability as a protector.

Murmuring a general good-night, she clumped her way to her bedroom, the crutches thumping against the bare wood floor.

Feeling strangely deserted, Barbara trailed the men into the kitchen, opting to prepare the sandwiches so as to delay the inevitable.

When the men were lounging comfortably at the table, cans of beer in hand, thick sandwiches in front of them, Thack propelled Barbara to a chair by arching one eyebrow tauntingly. Her attempts at delay exhausted, she subsided in weary surrender.

"Thack tells me you have a hankerin' to explore a ghost town, Barbara." Josh's voice slid over her like sumptuous cream. When she let a nod suffice for an answer, he went on, "I understand that this is your first visit to Texas?"

About to give the silent reply again, Barbara hesitated. Thack's drilling stare warned her to keep her head still and open her mouth.

"Yes, Mr. Barnet, it is." Though her tone was free of inflection, Barbara flashed a resentful glance at Thack, who reflected it right back to her from behind narrowed lids.

A cynical smile was visible on Josh's thin lips before he hid it behind the raised beer can. Pondering on his smile, and the reason for it, Barbara's eyes widened in dawning horror. A swift glance at Thack's hardened features confirmed the suspicion growing in her mind.

Had both men misread her reaction? Skimming a glance from Thack to Josh, Barbara was convinced they had. Good grief! she thought, appalled. Thack and Josh believed that she was repelled by Josh's artificial limb! The realization was followed by another consideration—was Josh accustomed to receiving that kind of reaction? Barbara clenched her teeth to contain a shudder of compassion for the man. If Josh was already positive the sight of his disability had repelled her, she would not add insult to injury with a display of pity.

Determined to correct their erroneous assumption, Barbara relaxed against the ladder-backed chair and smiled easily at Josh.

"I know Thack thinks I'm silly and romantic, Mr. Barnet," she confided softly. "But, you see, I grew up enthralled by the mystique of the legendary Westerner. I was a sucker for every Western hero that Hollywood ever produced. The mere mention of the words 'ghost town' made me tingle all over." She gave Josh the slow smile that had devastated more than one admirer. "Do you think I'm silly, too?"

His soft laughter swirled around her like folds of velvet. "No, Barbara, I don't think you're silly." His sapphire eyes glowed from within. "I think you're very beautiful, and very smart." Raising the beer can, he tipped it in a silent toast to her, then drained it in three long swallows.

Relief and pleasure warming her face, Barbara jumped to her feet. "Can I get you another drink, Mr. Barnet?"

"I'd appreciate it, *Barbara*." He softly emphasized her name. "I'd also appreciate it if you'd called me J.B. the way the rest of my friends do." The glow deep in his eyes brightened as he shifted his gaze to Thack. "You could bring the golden one another beer, too," he suggested in an amused tone.

"The golden one!" Barbara's captivating laugh trilled in the confines of the narrow room. "An apt description, J.B.," she complimented, retrieving the beer from the fridge, then swinging back to the table.

You'll get these valuable benefits as a
Silhouette Desire subscriber:

—**4 Books Free**
—**Free Home Delivery and never miss a title**
—**Receive your books at least one month before they're
  in the stores.**

Send no money — clip and mail today to reserve your Silhouette
Desire home subscription.

"But one can't help but wonder if the glitter isn't a thin gilt coating."

Thack's features had begun to relax. At her taunting remark, his face locked up again. The eyes he shifted to J.B. were nearly black with annoyance.

A genuine smile softening the harsh line of his thin lips, J.B. met Thack's stare directly while aiming his response at Barbara.

"That's no gilt coating, Barbara." His smile grew to reach his eyes. "That is pure twenty-four-carat gold."

An emotion, very much like love, sprouted then expanded inside Barbara's chest. But it wasn't until much later, when she was alone, in her own room, in her own bed, in the dark, that she realized the word that best described her feelings for the dark man: simpatico.

Almost asleep, Barbara smiled dreamily. What she felt for J.B. was affection, not love. It was impossible to feel love for him—she barely knew the man. Besides which, she was already in love with Thack.

Six

She couldn't be in love with Thack!

The denial sprang into Barbara's mind upon waking early the following morning. Frowning at the faint glow of dawn beyond the window, she wondered foggily what had wakened her. Her frown deepened at the sound of a light rap against her door.

"Last call, Barb," Thack announced, clearing up the mystery. "Breakfast is on the table. If you're going with me you'd better roll out."

Even with his stiff-legged gait on the bare plank floor, Barbara couldn't detect a sound as he moved away from her door.

Does the man have sponge soles on his boots? she grumbled to herself, tossing back the summer-weight blanket and stumbling to her feet. Standing by the bed she stretched languidly and yawned widely. Lord, she was sleepy!

The realization of why she was so sleepy jolted Barbara awake. She was tired simply because she'd spent most of the night grappling with the problem of her emotional aberration!

She *had* to be suffering culture shock or something. That could be the only explanation for the ridiculous idea that had sprung from some dark subterranean channel of her consciousness! She liked him, Barbara admitted to herself, but she couldn't be in love with him—could she?

The argument raged inside Barbara's head as she made her bed, completed her morning rituals, and dressed in a smart, swirl-patterned sports outfit of lipstick-red and buttercup-yellow.

It was not until she was stashing a fresh pack of cigarettes into her shoulder bag that Barbara realized that she had gotten through the majority of the previous day on the few cigarettes that had been in the crumpled pack she'd had in the car.

How odd, she mused, checking the butterfly clip anchoring the loose knot in her hair before leaving the room. Weeks before, when she'd realized she was smoking nearly two packs a day, she had started to monitor the number and had managed to cut back to a little more than one pack. Yet, if her calculations were correct, she had smoked less than half a pack the day before, and most of those before Thack arrived at the house—and he hadn't displayed disapproval by word or expression!

Come to that, her aunt hadn't smoked more than two cigarettes after lunch either! Barbara paused midway through the living room to shake her head in wonder. It was more than odd. It was downright weird!

Still frowning in consternation, Barbara continued on into the kitchen, and came to an abrupt stop.

Thack was not there. Ellie was sitting at the table sipping cautiously at the steaming coffee in the cup cradled in her hands. J.B. was standing at the stove, upon which rested several pans of various size.

"Pancakes or eggs, Barbara?" J.B. asked as she came to her gaping stop.

"Er, ah, pancakes, I guess." Barbara's frown deepened. As she walked to the table, she arched a quizzical brow at her aunt. Ellie smiled and shrugged.

"Bacon or sausage?" J.B.'s question drew Barbara's gaze back to the stove just as he expertly flipped a golden brown pancake onto a plate. While she watched, fascinated, he flipped a second then a third into a neat stack.

"Bacon, please." Bemused by his dexterous performance, she sank onto a chair.

"You got it." His actions swift and spare, J.B. transferred bacon onto the plate, then whipped around to cross to the table. As he slid the plate in front of her, a warm smile lifted the corners of his thin lips.

"Good morning," he murmured. "Would you like coffee, juice or both?" High spirits sparkled in his sapphire eyes.

Barbara smiled back. "Both, please, and good morning to you, too." Lowering her eyes, she swept her gaze over the expertly prepared meal. "It looks delicious," she complimented. A teasing light brightened her eyes. "Is cooking one of the duties you perform for Thack when he's at his ranch?"

"In comparison to Thack, he's a rank amateur," Thack drawled from the doorway. "And not only at the stove, either."

A feeling of unease slid along Barbara's spine. For all its softness, Thack's tone had an underlining thread of steel. Her gaze sought his face as he crossed to the table. Her breath caught in her throat at the sight of his set features and the cold expression in his eyes. Whatever was the matter with him? she wondered, watching him stare at J.B.

The smile had deserted J.B.'s thin lips, leaving them in a straight forbidding line. His lowered lids and short spiky lashes concealed his eyes. His lean body had grown taut.

"You find something wrong with the truck—*boss*?" The emphasis he'd placed on the address was chilling.

"No." Thack's gaze drilled into J.B. "I find something wrong with rustlers . . . of any sort."

Barbara was completely lost. Was Thack thinking about the man who'd shot him? But, if so, why glare at J.B.? If Barbara was confused, J.B. obviously was not. His lashes lifted fractionally to reveal glittering dark blue eyes. Then he sighed softly and moved his shoulders in a fatalistic shrug.

"Got the property fenced, eh?" A cynical smile twisted his lips. "And the wire's barbed." He nodded his head once. "I've gotten the message."

Thack's smile eased the tension in his facial muscles. "I figured you would." He sliced a quick glance at Barbara, then back to J.B. "Another time, friend," he murmured, easing onto the chair next to Barbara's. "And another woman."

Barbara was still gritting her teeth to contain her fury as the truck bounced along the road to the highway.

Another time and another woman! Thack had been warning J.B. to stay away from her! Pain shot into her

jaw from the force of her grinding teeth. How dare he?
And why, for heaven's sake? J.B. had made no over-
tures. He had been pleasant and rather sweet, nothing
more. Surely there was no reason for Thack to get all
uptight and jealous about that?

Jealous! Thack? Barbara's teeth unclenched as her
jaw dropped. No. Thack couldn't possibly be jealous—could he? It didn't make sense. But then, neither
did the ridiculous idea of her being in love with him.

As unobtrusively as possible, Barbara studied Thack
out of the corner of her eye. He was too attractive, too
easygoing, too damned sexy! Her gaze skimmed the
strong, capable hands gripping the steering wheel and
the muscled arms exposed by his short-sleeved shirt.
The sight of the golden column of his throat almost in-
terfered with her breathing. Her eyes strayed to his
profile, then skittered back to the windshield. He was
so delicious looking, she ached to nibble and taste.

"Have you decided?"

Though his voice was low, Barbara jerked as if from
a whiplash. "Decided?" She turned to frown at him; it
wasn't easy, he was so beautiful. "Decided what?"

"What to do about me." His gaze shifted from the
empty road to slide over her like warm satin.

"Do?" Barbara swallowed, and blamed the dryness
in her throat on the arid Texas climate. "Ah, what do
you mean, *do*?"

His quiet laughter danced along her nerves. "You
know exactly what I mean," he taunted. "You can't
decide whether to make love with me or murder me."

"That's not true!" Barbara denied. But of course it
was. "I—I haven't thought about it one way or the
other," she lied.

"Uh-huh." Thack moved his right hand from the wheel to her knee, then slowly glided his palm up her bare thigh. His laughter deepened at the tremor she couldn't repress. "I wanted to take you to bed from the first moment I set eyes on you," he admitted candidly. "And you know it." His hand moved again and Barbara jumped at the intimate caress of his fingers—jumped, but didn't move away.

"Thack, stop it!" Her voice lacked conviction. A low moan shuddered through her lips as his fingers stroked. The air-conditioner was throwing frigid air, but Barbara was suddenly so hot, so very hot, and so very helpless against his touch—damn him!

"You don't really want me to stop." Thack's voice was almost harsh with need. "Unless it's to stop by the side of the road." With a final caress he reluctantly returned his hand to the wheel. "Umm, ah, damn!" Thack breathed in sharply, unevenly. "Decide soon. Or you just might have to murder me to put me out of my misery."

Barbara shivered; with his hand no longer touching her, she quickly grew cold. What in the world was happening to her? She'd never reacted to a man this way, not even Peter. And she *had* been in love with him!

A flashing vision formed of a handsome dark man, then was as swiftly replaced by the visage of a man with brown eyes and white-gold hair. Barbara's breathing grew shallow. Damn Thackery Sharp!

"What's the struggle about, honey?" Thack's voice was back to normal. "I want to make love to you. You want to make love to me. We're both consenting adults. Why are you holding back?" The glance he shot her held genuine confusion.

Barbara bristled at his casual attitude. Peter's attitude to lovemaking had been casual, too. She'd been that route, she could not go it again. She wanted him, yes, but not enough to deal with the emotional consequences.

"I—I can't, Thack." Denying him hurt, badly.

The truck gained speed as Thack pressed his foot on the accelerator. "What do you mean, you can't?" he demanded.

"I do *not* sleep around," she gritted angrily.

"Damn!" Thack stamped on the brake, bringing the truck to a screeching halt. "I never thought you did!" He turned on the benchseat to glare at her. "But I *did* think you were a mature woman." He raked a hand through his hair, ruffling the neatly brushed waves. "How old are you? Twenty-two? Twenty-three?"

"Twenty-nine," Barbara confessed softly, avoiding his stare.

"You're kidding." Thack narrowed his eyes as he examined her face. "You don't look it. You act more like twenty."

Barbara raised her eyes to glare at him. "I do not act like a twenty-year-old! And I work at not looking my age. My income depends on my not looking my age. My entire career depends on my not looking my age!"

"And your career is very important to you." There was an odd, tired note in his tone.

"Well, of course it's important!" For some reason, Barbara felt defensive.

"Of course." Thack sighed. "I've heard that song before."

Barbara was on the point of demanding an explanation for his cryptic remark when he startled her with the abruptness of his action. Cursing under his breath, he grabbed his Stetson from the seat, tossed it onto the ledge in back, then reached for her, dragging her to him.

"Just what I needed, another *career girl*," he muttered an instant before he ground his mouth against hers.

Barbara knew she should ask him what he meant, she also knew she should be struggling and protesting his rough treatment. She also knew she wasn't going to do any of those things, simply because she was too busy returning the kiss that was swiftly progressing from merely hot to incendiary. Her lips parted at the nudge of his tongue, and she shivered in response to the urgent thrust into her mouth.

Her fear of emotional devastation faded into insignificance. Right here, right now, became paramount. Needing more of him, Barbara speared her fingers into his hair, loving the silky feel of the strands sliding between her fingers almost as much as she loved the silky brush of his mustache against her skin.

A growl vibrating his throat, Thack shoved her back against the seat and crushed her breasts with his chest. "Now tell me no, damn you," he groaned, taking her lower lip between his teeth. Clasping his broad hands to either side of her face, he held her still while he stroked her sensitive lips with his tongue. "God, I want you!" The intensity of his need seemed to surprise him. Moving carefully because of his injury, he eased his left leg over both of hers.

"Thack!" Barbara gasped as he gently lowered his body to straddle hers, then arched responsively as he aligned their hips.

"Barb, honey, you know you want it as much as I do. Let me have you, love." The softness of his tone contrasted excitingly with the hardness of his body. The thrust and stroke of his tongue destroyed the last of her resistance. She was sighing in surrender when the sound of squealing brakes and the blare of a horn pierced the steamy fog of sensuality clouding her mind. Thack slid his lips from hers, a scowl drawing his eyebrows together, when a hooting shout penetrated the closed window of the truck.

"Way to go, Thack!" Laughter followed the encouraging words.

Barbara pulled her hands from his hair and then stiffened in mortification. Moving too swiftly in the confining interior of the pickup, Thack scraped his spine on the dashboard as he twisted around and away from her. Cursing vehemently, he rolled the side window down and glared at the grinning face of a young man hanging halfway out of the four-wheel-drive vehicle that had been brought to a stop alongside the pickup. Another face peered at them from over the young man's shoulder.

"You guys getting off on playing peeping Tom now?" The unleashed fury in Thack's voice wiped the laughter from the two faces.

"Hey, Thack! We didn't mean anything!" the teenager hanging out of the window protested. The other young man jerked back, out of Thack's sight. "We're buddies, ain't we?" The kid was turning beet red. "We didn't think you'd get mad!"

"You didn't think—period," Thack snapped.

"Well, hell!" He gnawed his lip. "But if you're gonna make out—"

"That's enough, Billy!" Thack roared as he shoved the cab door open. The four-wheel drive's engine revved loudly as Thack thrust his left leg from the cab. "I think you idiots owe the lady an apology," he said grimly, cursing under his breath as he slid his injured leg across the seat.

Observing the exchange in silence, Barbara was caught between embarrassment and amusement. In fairness, she had to admit that she and Thack deserved some of the blame. Compassion welled for Billy as she watched his face pale in time to Thack's movements as he alighted from the pickup.

"Okay, Thack!" Billy thrust one hand out as if to halt Thack's progress. "Hey, lady, me and Cole are sorry! Okay?" he yelped. "Will you call him off— please?" Billy's eyes grew wider by the second.

"Thack." Pitched low, Barbara's tone carried both a plea and a demand. Wondering why Cole didn't simply stomp on the gas pedal, Barbara softly coaxed, "Get back in the truck, please, Thack."

He hesitated, and in that moment of stillness, Barbara could see Thack's shoulders ripple from the anger held inside his tall body. Then the tension eased from him, and Barbara released the breath she hadn't realized she was holding. Billy's expression revealed intense relief.

"Okay, you clowns, hit the pike—at or below the speed limit," Thack ordered in an ominous tone. "But fair warning," he added softly. "You give me any more grief, and you'll both be wearing your teeth around your necks on a chain. Do you read me?"

"Yes, sir!" Billy squeaked.

"Loud and clear!" Cole shouted from behind the wheel.

An instant later the vehicle moved away at a sedate pace, affording Barbara the time to read the banner pasted to the bumper. She was still staring at the departing vehicle as Thack slid back onto the seat.

"'I'm a roper not a doper,'" she quoted the words on the sticker. Frowning, she glanced at Thack. "What does that mean?" Her voice trailed away as she finished speaking; Thack's shoulders were still rippling, but now, observing him up close, she realized that he was shaking with silent laughter! He hadn't been furious with the boys at all! Thack was nearly falling apart with amusement!

"What?" he finally choked out as his laughter subsided.

Her own lips twitching, Barbara repeated the slogan. "What does it mean?" she asked again.

In control once more, Thack answered seriously. "Most of the young people out here are into rodeo," he explained. "They do their flying naturally, from the back of a horse."

"Good." Barbara's sobered tone held a wealth of conviction, much more than the average person displayed.

Thack sobered also. "Yes." He paused a moment, then probed carefully. "You've had a...a brush with drugs?"

"If you're asking if I've experimented, the answer is no," Barbara stated adamantly. "But I knew a girl, the sister of a...friend." Barbara grew quiet as an image formed in her mind of Peter's sister.

Sensing her withdrawal, Thack urged softly, "Go on."

Barbara blinked and looked away. "She was a model."

"Like you."

Laughing derisively, Barbara shifted her gaze back to him. "Not at all. Nicole was top drawer all the way. She came from a wealthy Philadelphia family. The Philadelphia Vanzants. Her father was a banker. Her older brother was a well-known power in both New York and Philly. She had her choice of the plum assignments simply because her face and body were so astonishingly perfect. Nicole was the most beautiful woman I've ever seen," Barbara concluded without a trace of envy.

Thack arched one white-gold brow. "Was?" he prompted. "She died?"

Barbara shook her head slowly. "No. At least not physically." A rush of tears stung her eyes. "Nicole was at the pinnacle of her career, soaring like a breathtaking, beautiful bird. I guess the atmosphere went to her head. She began to party all the time, with all the wrong people." A sigh wrenched her body. "She refused to listen to anyone, not even her brother. She was returning to New York from yet another wild party out on Long Island early one Sunday morning." Unconsciously, Barbara lowered her voice to a dry whisper. "The man driving the car was stoned out of his mind. Apparently he decided to go one-on-one with a sixteen-wheeler. He lost."

Barbara closed her eyes against the too vivid memory; *she* had been at the hospital that morning, had seen the destruction wrought by the senseless accident. Hot tears stung the backs of her eyelids. Her voice was thick when she continued.

"The driver and the other passenger in the car were killed instantly. Nicole hovered on the edge of life for weeks, and was hospitalized for months. The contusions, the fractures, the concussion all healed, eventually. But—" Barbara trembled visibly. "But there was scarring on her face and shoulders and, even though the doctors assured her that the scars would be very faint after cosmetic surgery, Nicole knew that her career was over, and she couldn't handle that."

The tears escaped her tightly closed lids, leaving a warm trail as they rolled down her face. Caught in the grip of memory, the image of Nicole's anguished face and haunted eyes pierced Barbara's heart as deeply as it had three years before.

The featherlight touch of Thack's fingers brushed away the image as well as the tears. "But she was alive, honey. Surely that was the most impor..." His voice trailed away as she shook her head sharply.

"No, Thack!" Sniffing, Barbara opened her tear-washed hazel eyes. "Not to Nicole. At first she was hysterical. Then she withdrew, at first psychologically, then, after she was released from the hospital, physically."

His gaze caressing her face as gently as his fingers had, Thack asked quietly, "What do you mean?"

"She ran away," Barbara replied simply. "Nicole's brother owned a house, a summer retreat somewhere along the coast of Maine. She went there to recuperate and never came back. I haven't seen her in years." Absently, unthinkingly, Barbara raised her hand to stroke his silky mustache. "Unlike your friend, J.B., who has obviously learned to live with his disability, Nicole simply ran away from it, and from her family and friends, too."

Thack had gone still at her touch, then tested the texture of her skin with the tip of his tongue. At the mention of J.B.'s name, he pulled back his head, severing the tingling connection between them.

"J.B.'s got his problems, too," he said tautly, turning to the steering wheel. "In his own way, he's run away, too. My ranch is J.B.'s 'retreat' from the world."

Tension simmered from him as he released the hand-brake on the idling truck.

Confused by his sudden abruptness, Barbara stared at him in wonder. What was he angry about? Was he impatient with her?

"Thack? What's the matter?"

"Nothing," he said flatly. "We'll never get to Ter-lingua at this rate." His explanation lacked conviction.

"But why are you angry?" Barbara persisted.

"I'm not." Thack's tone ended the discussion.

Thack *was* angry, though he hated to admit it, even to himself. He also knew why he was so angry. The emotion seething through him was caused by plain old-fashioned jealousy.

Rigidly controlling the urge to press the gas pedal to the floor with his foot, Thack kept his eyes straight ahead, steady on the deserted road, denying his senses the pleasure of drinking in the sight of the woman seated beside him.

What had happened to him within the last twenty-four hours? What had begun as a desire to appease a basic need had turned into a confusing jumble of tangled emotions, the uppermost at that moment being jealousy.

Who the hell needed this? he thought savagely. After finally getting his life back together since his divorce, he'd been doing just fine on his own. He didn't want the complications that went hand-in-hand with emotional involvement.

Dammit! All he'd wanted was to get laid! Thack's fingers tightened on the wheel. He hadn't counted on wanting more than the transient pleasure. But now, the

want, the need, went much deeper than the uncompli-
cated desire for a quick roll on a bed.

His overwhelming desire now was to possess, to protect, to *own*.... And who the hell did J.B. think he
was—eating Thack Sharp's woman with his damned
blue eyes!

Unable to resist the urge, Thack sliced a glance at
Barbara's profile, sliding his gaze from the disordered
topknot of brown-red hair, to the smoothness of her
brow, and down her short, straight nose to the enticing
fullness of her kiss-reddened lips. Biting back a curse,
he dragged his gaze to the windshield.

What was he doing here? Where was he going at a
frantically controlled forty-five miles an hour?

The question slammed into Thack with the force of
a physical blow. Never before in his life had he lost sight
of his objective—not even through the worst days with
his ex-wife, the sweet, avaricious Alice!

And, for an instant there, Thack realized that he had
actually forgotten where the hell he was going! Terlingua! Ellie's gold! The thieves! Jeez-us Christ all Fri-
day!

No. Oooh, no! A shudder tore through Thack's
body. Not again. The protest rang loudly inside his
head. He was sinking in the idiotic quagmire laugh-
ingly known as *love*, for God's sake! And the object of
his screwed-up emotions was yet another career girl—a
genuine New York model, of all things!

Thack's knuckles turned white as his grip tightened
on the wheel. He was most assuredly in big trouble.

"Are—are we almost there?"

Thack's entire body jerked at the tentative, almost
fearful note in Barbara's usually attractive voice.

God, had he frightened her? *Was* he frightening her still with his tense and unsociable behavior? Chagrin was evident on the curve of his lips as he offered her a hesitant smile.

"I want you, Barbara," Thack whispered in a tone made rough with need, then ground his teeth at her choking gasp. *Good goin', Sharp,* he thought disgustedly. *If she raps you in the mouth, you'll know you deserve it!*

Barbara didn't rap Thack in the mouth; she punched him on his upper arm.

"Stop saying that, Thack!" she ordered in a pleading tone.

The blow from her soft hand glanced off of Thack's arm, but tickled his funny bone. Laughing softly, he slanted a devilish look at her, arching one eyebrow at the sight of her trembling fingers as she lit up a cigarette—her first since entering the pickup.

Ignoring the spontaneous hunger triggered by the scent of burning tobacco, Thack responded honestly. "Ah, hell, honey, I *do* want you. Not saying it doesn't change it."

"Well, I don't want to hear it anymore," Barbara retorted. "And stop swearing, too!" she added irritably, drawing deeply on the cigarette. "Do you realize how often you swear?"

"Do you realize how often you smoke?" Thack responded mildly, grinning at the indignant expression on her beautiful face.

"Well, ah, dammit, Thack! There's no comparison between the two!" Barbara sputtered, glaring at him.

Thack roared. Throwing his head back, he let the laughter pour out of him, and with it all his tensions. Bump it, he thought, deciding to ride with the tide. If he was falling in love—well, no ifs about it, he *was* falling in love—then he'd take whatever Barbara allowed him to have—good, bad, or indifferent.

"You're picking up my bad habit of swearing, sweetheart," he teased, still chuckling. "Now, with any luck at all, maybe you'll pick up my urge to merge."

"Thackery Sharp, I'm warning you!"

For all the sting in her tone, Thack caught the underlying amusement. His laughter rang out again. Damned if he didn't feel great all of a sudden.

Removing his right hand from the wheel, he reached toward her. Catching her around the shoulders, he tugged her across the seat to him. The sensations created by her breast pressing against his side felt great, too.

"You're crazy, you know that?" Tilting her head back against his hard shoulder, Barbara gazed up at Thack in bemusement. His only response was a lopsided grin and the tightening of his arm.

Sighing with a contentment that she absolutely refused to examine, Barbara snuggled into the hard strength of his body. Immediately a problem arose to torment her. How was she supposed to relax when her entire body tingled from the electric current that was pulsating through her from the contact of her breast with his chest?

"God, I love it!" Thack groaned, his arm flexing. "But it sure plays hell with my concentration."

Disappointed, Barbara stirred and began to move away. Thack hauled her back forcefully. "No! Don't move, honey. I'll bite the bullet and bear the agony." Dipping his head, he brushed his lips over her brow, muttering, "Hell, I'll eat the damned bullet if you'll just stay put."

Turning her head, Barbara gently sank her teeth into his muscular shoulder.

"Ouch!" Thack barked. "What was that for?"

"Swearing." She glanced up at him from under her lashes. "I'll make a deal with you, Thack," she said seriously. "I'll cut down on the cigarettes if you'll cut down on the swearing." She raised her eyebrows tauntingly, challengingly.

Thack didn't hesitate a second. "You've got a deal, sweetheart," he agreed, grinning like a boy let out of school.

Seven

The ghost town of Terlingua was a disappointment for Barbara. It consisted of a smattering of squat, square, flat-topped buildings that she assumed were adobe. One structure, larger than the others, actually boasted a sloped tin roof.

The terrain surrounding the cluster of buildings was desolate and as flat as the roofs, except for some low mounds of sandy earth that reminded Barbara of sand dunes.

As they approached the town over an uneven dirt road, Thack angled his head at her to catch her reaction to the place. Unknowingly, Barbara's disenchantment with Terlingua fulfilled his expectations.

"This is it?" Barbara's gaze slowly scanned the remains of what had been an active mercury mining center. "This is Terlingua?"

"This is it." Thack raised a cloud of dust as he brought the pickup to a stop. "I *did* tell you it wasn't much." Reaching back, he plucked his hat from the ledge, then settled it on his head.

Wasn't much? Barbara glanced around bleakly as she stepped down from the truck, wincing at the blast of heat that hit her like a blow. It wasn't anything! Had people actually lived, worked and thrived here? Barbara sighed her disappointment; so much for her youthful fantasies of what a ghost town looked like.

Circling the front of the truck, Thack came to stand beside her, an understanding smile curving his lips. "Young dreams die hard, don't they?" he murmured sympathetically.

"Do they exist anywhere," she wonder aloud, "the towns of my dreams?"

"Does reality ever measure up to our dreams?" Thack answered with a question.

A sad little smile shadowed Barbara's lips. "No, I suppose not." How many times did she have to prove the truth of his assertion? she asked herself, her eyes skimming over the deserted environs of yet another shattered illusion. Modeling had been one of the glamorous dreams that had faded in the glaring light of reality. Peter Vanzant had been the most painful disappointment of all. Terlingua didn't really hurt, it just ached a little.

"Come on." Clasping her hand in his, Thack tugged her into motion. "Let's play tourist and have a look around." One white-gold brow peaked as he glanced down at her. "Or have you forgotten why we're here?"

Barbara frowned up at him. "But surely you don't really expect to find the thieves here?" Shifting her gaze, she scowled at the area dismissively. "There's *nothing* here!"

Thack ambled off, bringing her with him. "You never can tell," he mused, his narrow-eyed glance belying his casual attitude.

Raising her eyes heavenward, Barbara scuffed along beside him, wiggling her toes to dislodge the dirt that was getting into her sandals.

"Someone's been here, and recently, too."

"What?" Barbara was too involved with ruing her choice of footgear that morning; his observation went right by her.

"Damn!" Not bothering to reply, Thack turned and quickly limped back to the pickup, practically dragging her with him.

"Thack!" Barbara protested, pulling at his hand in an unsuccessful bid for freedom. "Have you flipped? What are you doing?"

He released her so abruptly she nearly fell over. "What I should have been doing all along." Swinging the passenger door open, he leaned into the cab of the pickup, stretching one arm out to pull a rifle from the mounted gun rack. "I'm beginning to think." Reaching to the ledge behind the seat he grasped a box of shells.

Barbara backed up slowly as he withdrew from the cab. "Wh—what are you going to do with that?" Her wide-eyed gaze clung to the long-barreled weapon.

"Keep it tightly in my fist," Thack muttered, shoving shells into the chamber, "where it belongs."

The rifle was spotless and gleamed in the relentless glare of sunlight; Barbara thought it was as ugly as sin. She took another step back. "But why?" she swallowed the arid taste of fear and glanced around nervously. "Are there snakes?"

Thack tossed the cartridge box onto the seat and slammed the door shut. "Of the two-legged variety." Capturing her hand again, he began walking toward a short row of boxlike buildings. "Stay close, honey." There was an edge to his voice that she hadn't heard before. Barbara decided immediately that she didn't like it. "They're here," he went on, too calmly. "I can feel it in my bones."

What had she gotten herself into here? Uneasiness cooled her sweat-slick skin as they approached the first of the cubical structures. When Thack suddenly released her hand, then stepped in front of her, Barbara began to shiver with apprehension.

"Tha—"

"Shss." Thack's silencing hiss caused a skip in her heart beat. "Stay put."

Frozen to the spot, Barbara watched as Thack, right index finger curled around the rifle's trigger, drifted as soundlessly as smoke to the recessed doorway. There was an instant's hesitation, then he moved with a speed that stole her breath. Raising the rifle to his shoulder, Thack dashed into the small building. Barbara steeled herself for the burst of gunfire that never came. The scene was replayed at each doorway.

They were approaching the last building when the growling sound of an engine revving to life shattered the silent tension. In the hot, still air, it was difficult for Barbara to ascertain from which direction the sound had come; not so for Thack.

A curse rumbling in his throat, Thack's head snapped up, his gaze fixed on a larger building beyond the row of cubicals. At that exact moment a battered truck careened around the building and the report from a rifle cracked the heavy atmosphere. In stunned bewilderment, Barbara stared at the furrow the bullet had dug in the earth less than two feet from where she and Thack stood.

Then, Barbara went flying, Thack's snarled curses ringing in her ears as he shoved her forcefully through the opening in the boxlike building. She had a flashing image of the battered truck bearing down on them an instant before she landed with a jarring thud on the hard-packed earth floor. Gasping to regain the breath that had been knocked out of her, Barbara stared in horror as Thack stepped into the doorway, dropped to one knee, and positioned the rifle against his shoulder all in a single fluid move.

Thack was clearly outlined in the narrow doorway, a sitting duck for whoever was shooting at them from inside the truck. His vulnerability gave Barbara a frightening reason for her next, almost reflex, action.

Rolling into a crouch, she scurried across the floor and threw her body into his, knocking him sideways out of the doorway. Even in her dazed bemusement, Barbara heard the roars that rent the air simultaneously.

There was the roar of the truck's engine as it veered to the left a few yards from the building and sped away with tires screeching. There was the roar from the rifle as Thack, jostled by Barbara, squeezed the trigger. There was a roar of startled surprise from Thack's throat in the form of an explicitly colorful expletive.

The momentum created by Barbara's body slamming into Thack's carried her out of the building with him. They tumbled in the gritty dirt in a tangle of arms, legs, and sweaty bodies as the truck tore away from the scene.

When they stopped moving, Barbara found herself face down in the dirt with Thack's long frame on top of her.

Choking on the dirt, Barbara shook her head, spitting the dust from her mouth and sputtering invectives at Thack. She was less than articulate.

"Get...off me...you...you...great, ah, ox!" She exhaled deeply as his weight was removed. "You—you've got to weigh a ton!" she croaked, dragging air into her body.

Panting, Barbara flipped onto her back and stared up at Thack. His palms planted on either side of her, his torso supported by stiffened arms, Thack was staring at the truck, diminishing in the distance. To her amazement, a smile of satisfaction lifted the corners of his lips.

"Would you tell me what's so darned funny?" she demanded, expelling a harsh breath.

"Besides you?" Thack lowered his gaze to her eyes. "Those stupid jerks are headed right for Big Bend," he explained, his gaze skimming over her face in a thorough examination. "Are you all right?"

"Oh, I'm fine," Barbara muttered sarcastically. "Unless you consider the crushing weight on my body and the dirt in my mouth!"

Thack had the gall to laugh. "You brought it on yourself." His laughter ceased abruptly. "Why the hell did you do that?" he asked in a deceptively cool tone.

"Why? Why!" Barbara screeched, outraged. "Because I didn't want to see you murdered!" Shouting hurt her dry throat, yet she continued. "Do you have some kind of death wish or something?"

His brown eyes appearing to melt, Thack mutely shook his head while lowering it to hers. "No," he murmured, sexily—very sexily. "But I do have a sudden yen to discover what dirt tastes like."

Dipping his head, he covered her parted lips with his own. For a moment, a very brief moment, Barbara's mind was filled with the incongruity of his action. They were lying in the dirt in a deserted ghost town, for heaven's sake! Was this man a sex maniac, completely crazy, or what?

The invasion of Thack's hungry tongue dissolved Barbara's instant of lucidity. As he shifted his body into the cradle of her thighs, awareness of his arousal shocked her senses and fired her blood. Following an instinctive urge older than time, she coiled her arms around his muscle-tautened neck, returning his kiss as greedily as it was offered. Within seconds, the heat generated by the harsh Texas sun paled in comparison to the blast furnace raging inside Barbara.

When Thack slid his mouth from hers, she moaned a low protest, then gasped with delight as he left a trail of stinging kisses down the arched column of her throat.

"God, you taste good," Thack murmured against her moist skin, "even coated with dust." Very slowly, he lowered his chest to gently crush her breasts, and rotated his hips into hers.

"Thack!" Barbara cried out, reacting to the sensations his undulating hips sent sizzling to the lower half of her body. Unthinkingly, she encircled his thighs with her legs. Drawing his breath in sharply, Thack responded by thrusting his body against hers.

Though his dust-powdered jeans abraded the smooth, sensitive skin on the insides of her thighs, Barbara tightened the embrace of her arms and legs and sought the sweetness of his mouth with her tingling lips.

"Barb." Thack groaned her name against her lips, and rocked his hard body into the softness of hers. "Honey! God, I want you so badly! But not here." His breathing ragged, he moved his weight from her, rolling onto his back and flinging one arm over his eyes to block out the sunlight...or something. He breathed in deeply several times before positioning his arm above his head and turning to gaze into her passion-brightened eyes. "When I make love to you, I want it to be perfect," he whispered. "I want more for us than a quick clutch and grapple in the dust."

Fully aware of the promise in his words, Barbara stared into the dark depths of Thack's eyes as her breathing returned to normal. Strangely, instead of feeling shame, humiliation or embarrassment for her uninhibited response to him, she was filled to overflowing with a delicious sense of elation.

"And what if it isn't perfect?" she whispered, not bothering to refute his remark. "What then?"

Moving with a swiftness that Barbara was becoming used to, Thack leaned close to brush his lips over hers. "I guess you'll just have to shoot me," he replied solemnly.

Barbara looked stunned for an instant, then she burst out laughing. "You really are crazy, aren't you?" Shaking her head, she pushed on his shoulders. "And stop grinning at me like an idiot! Haul your backside off the ground and help me up," she commanded imperiously.

Although he laughed delightedly, Thack nevertheless got up, then pulled Barbara to her feet and directly into his arms.

"You know what, Barbara Holcomb?" he asked softly, imprisoning her in the loose circle of his arms.

"No. What?" Barbara answered, feeling her heart thump into overdrive.

"I think I'm beginning to like you as much as I want you." His smile was endearingly uncertain. "Do you like me, too?"

Barbara was lost—heart, soul and mind. "Yes, Thackery Sharp, I like you, too. Very much." Her insides melted as he swallowed with obvious difficulty.

"And?" he prodded hopefully.

"And I want you." Barbara gave him the honesty he was asking of her. Leaning forward, she rested her forehead on his chest, taking courage from the rapid thud of his heartbeat. "Thack, I'm not very good at this," she admitted tremulously. "There has been only one man, and that ended three years ago." Involved in untangling her own emotions, Barbara was beyond understanding the one that suddenly accelerated his heart rate. "When it comes to intimate relationships, I'm pretty much a twenty-nine-year-old dumb-dumb." She attempted a small laugh, and failed.

The loose circle of Thack's arms closed around her comfortingly. His lips trailed through her mussed hair on a path to her ear. "I guess I'd better admit that I'm glad to hear that you're not very good at this." The tip of his tongue teased the outer curl of her ear. "Don't worry, honey. I won't rush you. We'll just let it happen when it happens," he promised, gliding his lips to the corner of her mouth. "Okay?" His warm breath caressed her lips.

Barbara was finding it hard to breathe again. With a fractional move she slid her mouth over his. "Should *I* admit that it's happening now?" she asked in a husky gasp.

"Barb, honey! Don't do this to me." Releasing his hold, Thack stepped back, his eyes still gazing at her hungrily. "I gotta get you out of here—" he smiled, shakily "—before I do something really stupid."

"You mean, before *we* do something really stupid." With her acceptance of shared responsibility, Barbara returned his shaky smile.

Thack didn't miss the meaning behind her words. His smile growing warm, he held out his hand, leading her to the pickup after she slid her palm trustingly into his.

The interior of the cab felt like an oven. The heated leather seat scorched the backs of Barbara's thighs. Her expression eloquent, she carefully eased her bottom onto the seat.

An instant after he turned on the engine, Thack flicked the air-conditioner switch to full blast.

"It'll cool off in a few minutes," he assured her ruefully.

Nodding, Barbara closed her eyes and rested her head against the seat.

"Tired?"

"Yes." An apologetic smile curved her lips. "The heat and the excitement I suppose." Barbara knew she didn't have to elaborate on which form of excitement she was referring to; Thack's soft chuckle made it clear he understood perfectly.

"Come over here." Looping his arms around her shoulders he coaxed her across the seat, settling her neatly against his side.

Even with the bump and jostle of the truck over the dirt road, Barbara was asleep within minutes. The cessation of movement woke her. "Where are we?" Barbara frowned.

"In Tortilla." Thack pulled on the hand brake and, with a final hug, lifted his arm from her shoulders. "About twenty-eight miles out of Terlingua."

Her eyes dull with sleep, Barbara glanced around at the smattering of buildings. There weren't as many as in the ghost town they'd just left.

"Tortilla is a town?" Barbara asked bleakly, returning her gaze to him.

Thack laughed. "Well, sort of. It started out as a diner and gas station two enterprising folks opened here in hopes of catching some of the tourist trade in and out of Big Bend. The name of the diner was Tortilla," Thack motioned to an unattractive structure to their left. A long, hand-painted sign above the door read Tortilla Diner. "Not long after the diner and gas station went into business, a few other folks settled." His hand moved to indicate several other buildings. "An eager young couple opened the motel, on the assumption that the tourists would welcome a bed to sleep in after roughing it in the park." His teeth flashed whitely in the afternoon sunlight. "They were right, too. Then a middle-aged couple went into business with that dry goods-souvenir store over by the motel. Next an ambitious Mexican-American opened the cantina on the other side of the motel and, whoa, boy, instant town. The full name of the place is Tortilla Junction, but nobody uses it."

"And this is the town your contacts told you had been visited by raiders?" Barbara asked musingly.

Thack nodded. "The town and the few shoestring ranches that have sprung up around it."

"Ummm," Barbara murmured. "And that's why we've stopped here? So you can find out more information about the thieves?"

"No." Thack smiled into her look of surprise. "I know where the thieves are, or at least I think I know."

"The Big Bend?"

"Yeah." Thack chuckled. "Those three are just about stupid enough to high tail it to the hills." His chuckle deepened. "I'm just stupid enough to go in there after them. And that's why we're here. I'm going to outfit myself for a few days in the mountains, and find someone to drive you back to Ellie's ranch."

"No!" The protest burst from Barbara, before she even thought about it. She was no longer reasoning, but obeying emotional dictates. "Thack, please, don't send me back," she said urgently before he could speak. "Let me go with you."

Thack was shaking his head even as she made her plea. "Too dangerous, honey. Those men are armed, and feeling desperate by now." Reaching out, he drew a tingling line down her cheek with his fingers. "I just found you, I'm not taking any chances on losing you."

Barbara was much too agitated to understand the commitment woven into his refusal. All she heard *was* the refusal. She heard it, and fought it.

"I won't go back. You can't make me go back," she declared obstinately. "I just found you, too," she went on pleadingly when his face hardened. "Thack, please, let me stay with you."

"Oh, Barb." Thack sighed and ran a hand around the back of his neck. He was weakening, and he knew it. Barbara knew it, too.

"I won't be any trouble," she promised. "I'll do exactly what you tell me to do, when you tell me to do it." By this point, Barbara was fully conscious of what she was saying and of what she was implying. She knew she was going to give herself to Thack, without strings, without demands and, hopefully, without regret. With a ruthlessness she hadn't known she was capable of, she buried the qualms arising from her ingrained code of conduct, a feat she had not been able to accomplish in the entire time she'd spent with Peter.

Aware, and willing to accept whatever Thack offered her, for however long he offered it, Barbara added strength to her argument. "Thack, I have a career and a life back east that I'll have to return to very soon. I want to stay with you now." She didn't touch him, except with her imploring gaze. "Take me with you. I promise I'll be good."

Thack gnawed on the ends of his mustache with his bottom teeth, the battle raging inside evident in his eyes. Then he exhaled harshly. Dammit! He didn't want to send her back to Ellie's ranch. He wanted her with him. Besides, J.B. was at Ellie's place. Thack knew it was the final consideration that clinched it—and him.

"You'll obey my commands instantly and without argument?" It was a token question, he acknowledged ruefully, a question designed to ease his conscience more than elicit compliance from Barbara.

"Instantly, without argument," she repeated assuringly.

He held out a moment longer, then after promising himself he'd protect her with his own life if necessary, Thack relented.

"All right, I'll take you with me." Then, before she could voice the words of thanks hovering on her lips, he tacked on roughly, "But I'm warning you, Barb. If I yell move, you had better do it."

Barbara didn't say thanks, she didn't *say* anything. With an unintelligible cry, she flung herself against him, grasping his head to draw his mouth to hers. The ensuing kiss was very brief, but extremely hot.

"Ah...yeah," Thack muttered, reluctantly lifting his head. "I think we'd better cool it before we draw a crowd." His movements charmingly uncoordinated, he pushed the door open.

Barbara couldn't contain the laughter that rippled from her throat. "Draw a crowd? Here?" She gazed pointedly at the solitary car parked in front of the diner.

Stepping out of the truck, Thack glanced back to grin at her. "All right," he drawled, his eyes wickedly enticing. "We'd better cool it before you draw out the animal in me."

"Animal?" Sliding across the seat to exit from his side of the pickup truck, she grinned back at him. "A teddy bear."

Affecting a scowl, Thack caught her close after she jumped from the cab of the truck. "You want to hear me growl?" Bending his head swiftly he nipped on her ear.

"Thack!" Barbara admonished, grasping his shirt-front to steady her suddenly weak legs. The weakness intensified when his lips teased at her earlobe.

God it was hot! Her breath coming in short little puffs, Barbara tried to blame the searing heat on the Texas climate. There was only one problem, the heat was being generated from within, not without.

"Thack, we're on a public street," she cautioned, moaning as he slipped the tip of his tongue into her ear.

Loosening the grip he had on her waist, Thack moved back. "I know, I know," he muttered, grabbing her hand and striding toward the diner. His long body was taut with frustration and suppressed desire thickened his voice. "Dammit! If I ever get you alone, I'll very likely keep you in bed for a solid week."

Barbara came to a dead stop, not because his muttered statement shocked her, but because it thrilled her. Anticipation surging through her system, she pulled at his tugging hand.

"Is that a promise?" she demanded softly when he paused to look back at her inquiringly.

A flame leaped brightly in the depths of his eyes, then was quickly banked. "Honey, feeling the way I do, I could easily promise you a full thirty-one-day month in the bed of your choice." His lips twisted into a grimace as he scanned the area with narrowed eyes. "But not in this poor excuse for a town." With a quick tug of his hand he brought her to him. "I've got a previous promise to your aunt to honor." Sighing, he drew her with him to the entrance to the diner. "After this crazy manhunt is over, you name the time and the place and I'll give you my undivided attention—and *that's* a promise." His hand hesitated on the door handle and he arched his brows at her. "Okay?"

Barbara could barely breathe, let alone speak. "Sounds fair to me," she finally managed in a dry whisper.

The smile began in his eyes, worked its way to his lips, then found its way into her heart. "Are you hungry?" Thack asked, caressing her features with a single gaze.

"What a question!" Barbara blurted out artlessly.

Laughter rumbled from his throat. "For food, darling!" Thack chided while laughing.

Barbara didn't even blush. "Oh, food," she shrugged, then frowned. "Yes, come to think of it, I am." Amazement colored her tone and widened her eyes. "We haven't eaten since breakfast, and now it's almost dinnertime!"

"I knew that," Thack drawled laconically. "That's why we're here taking up space at the door to this diner." He tilted his head at the building. "Shall we?"

The interior of the diner was a pleasant surprise. Though not at all elaborate, the decor was warmly homey. Once they were seated in a booth, Barbara ordered the dinner special of chicken-fried steak, while Thack opted for a large T-bone prepared, as he put it, "Not quite dead."

Encapsuled in a moody silence, they sipped on cold beer while waiting for their meals. Growing tense in the lengthening quiet, Barbara stared into the golden liquid in her glass. The lack of conversation was conducive to thought, which in turn opened the door to speculation.

What if Thack were married? Jolted by the sudden thought, and by her failure to consider such a possibility before offering herself to him, Barbara glanced up at him, her eyes shadowed with concern.

"What's the matter?" Thack frowned.

Barbara sipped at her beer, carefully set her glass down, then plunged. "You're not by any chance married, are you?" Holding her breath, she waited for his response. She didn't wait long.

"Married!" Thack's eyes flickered with incredulity. "Do I strike you as the unfaithful type?" His voice low, but harsh, he continued before she could reply. "No, I'm not married, or engaged, or seeing anyone on a regular basis, Barbara." Though he couldn't miss noticing her sigh of relief, his tone remained steely. "If I were *any* of the above I would not have touched you—" he exhaled raggedly "—at least not before I'd severed the relationship."

Barbara wasn't at all sure she cared for his last few words. Lowering her lashes, she stared into her glass. "You find it easy to sever relationships?" she asked unevenly.

"No, I don't find it easy to sever relationships," Thack denied roughly. "Dammit, Barbara, look at me."

His terse command brought her head up abruptly. Moistening her suddenly dry lips, Barbara faced the anger in his eyes.

"Listen very carefully, honey, because I'm only going to say this once." Thack's tone was devoid of inflection. "I outgrew indiscriminate sex before I reached the age of consent." A wry smile twisted his lips at the flush that tinged her cheeks. "I *was* married once. It lasted four years . . . four long, enlightening years. There have been no serious relationships since I paid through the nose for a divorce six years ago. There has been the occasional, ah, *friend*," he admitted sardonically. "I'm a man, with all the normal drives, but, as I am also particular, I indulge those drives discreetly and infrequently." The rough edge on his tone smoothed a little. "Now answer my question: *do* I strike you as the unfaithful type?" he asked tensely.

"No!" Barbara denied immediately. "But . . ."

"But what?" Thack prodded as her voice faded.

Feeling somewhat trapped, Barbara searched for words to explain her emotions without revealing too much of herself to him. The waitress was an unexpected ally. Arriving at their booth with their food, the pleasant young woman afforded Barbara a few minutes to compose herself.

"But what?" Thack demanded the moment the waitress finished serving them and moved away.

"Thack, you must admit that the attraction, or chemistry, or whatever it is between us, is rather overpowering," Barbara murmured. Thack nodded sharply, and grinned widely. Barbara bit on her lips before stumbling on. "Well, when an attraction is so...so very strong, it's easy to forget prior commitments in the heat of the moment, isn't it?"

"Maybe so," Thack conceded, then qualified, "But, had there been a prior commitment, I would not have touched you," he continued: "I still would have wanted to, but I wouldn't have."

There was not a thing casual or laid back about the man sitting across the booth from Barbara. Thack's stare was cool and direct, his tone steady and sincere.

"I'm something of a traditionalist, Barb. I believe in fidelity."

Barbara trembled from the release of inner tension. "I'm glad, Thack, because I believe in fidelity, too."

With a smile that curved his lips, the easygoing Thack returned, "I'm glad. You just confirmed my opinion of you."

At his teasing observation, Barbara realized how very little they really knew about one another. And, she thought starkly, she had practically agreed to having an affair with him!

"We don't know each other at all, do we?" Barbara voiced her thoughts while making a show of cutting the meat on her plate.

Reaching across the table, Thack halted her pointless action by covering her fingers with his broad palm. "We'll remedy that situation as soon as we've eaten and collected the gear we'll need," he said quietly.

A current of heat ran up Barbara's arm at his light touch. Not even attempting to conceal her tremor of response, she let the fork clatter from her tingling fingers.

"What do you mean?" she asked in a raspy whisper.

Thack's seductive smile promised . . . everything.

"It's pointless to go into the Big Bend today," he explained softly. "We have the entire night to get to know each other."

Eight

The motel room was clean and functional, not at all conducive to seduction. Standing just inside the door, Barbara surveyed her surroundings impassively.

Aside from the one double bed opposite the door, the furnishings consisted of a narrow chest of drawers, a molded-plastic chair, and a table-floor lamp, the table part of it boasting several scars and a single ashtray.

Pushing away from the door, Barbara crossed the worn carpet and dropped her armful of packages onto the bed. Directly after eating, Thack had steered Barbara to the dry goods store where, in addition to the clothes, stout walking boots and other supplies required for a trip into the Big Bend, she had purchased a singularly unattractive cotton nightgown, complete with long sleeves and a high-collared neckline. Other than the necessities, Thack had bought a bottle of overpriced inferior wine at the cantina.

"Loosens the tongue," he'd defended when she raised her eyebrows in question.

Now, away from Thack, Barbara was getting a little edgy. Uncertainty had set in when they'd entered the motel lobby.

"Hey, Thack, how's it goin'?" The man behind the registration desk called as Thack ushered her into the office.

"Don't pay to complain," Thack drawled.

During the ensuing exchange of pleasantries, Barbara was reminded of her aunt's assertion that just about everybody in West Texas knew Thack Sharp. Barbara concluded that Ellie had not been exaggerating in the least. Wondering about the footloose life-style of the man she was beginning to find herself in love with, Barbara was rudely brought to attention by the desk clerk's exclamation.

"What do you want two rooms for?" The clerk ran an assessing glance from her head to her sandaled feet, lingering on the long expanse of her legs.

Barbara had to fight an urge to step up to the desk and slap the suggestive smile from the man's lips. Thack didn't fight the urge, but he delivered the slap verbally.

"Get your slimy-eyed gaze off of her." Cold steel wouldn't have measured up to Thack's tone. "How well do you know me, Bobby?" Thack asked the man what Barbara considered an unrelated query.

Bobby wet his lips nervously, revealingly. "Ah, well, about as well as anybody else around here, Thack," he muttered. "Why?"

"Have I ever brought a woman to this place before?" Thack demanded in a frighteningly soft voice.

Bobby swallowed rapidly three times. "N–No."

"Does that suggest something to you?" Thack persisted.

"This, ah, lady is special?" Bobby looked a trifle green.

"This lady is *very* special, Bobby," Thack said, chillingly. "This lady is mine." Curling his arm around her waist, Thack drew her against his side. "I think you owe *my* lady an apology."

"I'm sorry, ma'am." Bobby said in a low voice. "I didn't mean any insult."

Standing at the foot of the bed, Barbara felt a flutter in her midsection as she remembered the cold deadliness that had emanated from Thack for those few minutes. It still had the power to chill her blood even though Thack had reverted to his easygoing self seconds after Bobby's apology.

Who was this man, and what was he really all about? Barbara asked herself nervously. One minute Thack was loose and easygoing, all golden bronze and laughing. Then, in an instant, he could change, becoming granite-hard and icy, his lips looking as if they'd never experienced the tug of a smile. And what was she doing, miles from the known and understood, with a man who could effortlessly fire her senses one moment then freeze her blood the next?

Barbara's glance skittered around the room, as if searching for a means of escape. In the back of her mind, a tiny voice scolded: you should have let him take you back to the ranch, to the safety of Aunt Ellie's more predictable eccentricity, and the protection afforded by the presence of one of Thack's friends.

But, would J.B. in fact protect her? Barbara had no doubt whatsoever that, under the usual circumstances, J.B. would protect her with his own life if necessary;

instinct assured her J.B. was the type of man who would protect any woman with his life. But the circumstances weren't usual. With a few seemingly innocuous words, Thack had issued a hands-off warning to J.B. with regard to Barbara. The way J.B. had backed away from a confrontation with Thack told the complete story; Thack was definitely calling the shots—if in a very soft voice.

So, where did that leave her? Gathering her reserve of strength, Barbara faced the answer. She was exactly where she'd placed herself—in a motel room miles from the familiar environs of tall spires and dirty streets. She was out of her element and floundering badly. She was scared and, yes, excited at one and the same time.

The muted sound of someone moving around in the room that was connected to hers drew Barbara from introspection. Thack! Good grief, he would be at her door, wine bottle in hand, in a very few minutes! His parting words as he'd unlocked her door, rang loudly in her head.

"I'll be here in thirty minutes, honey, showered, shaved, and ready for that conversation I promised you, or anything else you might want."

Scooping up the voluminous gown and the small container of shampoo she'd included in the pile of "essentials" for entering the Big Bend, Barbara dashed for the bathroom.

She was still in the bathroom, attempting to air-brush her towel-dried hair, when Thack tapped lightly on the door in the hall. The brush clattered to the floor from her nerveless fingers and she stared at the scrubbed-clean, makeup-free face reflected in the small mirror above the sink.

You look like yesterday's leftovers! Barbara told her image silently. Too used to seeing herself, she missed the shadow of vulnerability in her wide hazel eyes, the allure of the curve of her cheeks, the temptation of her naturally pink, sensuous lips, all framed by the mass of chestnut hair tumbling onto her shoulders and halfway down her back.

Thack, as a very interested observer, missed none of Barbara's rather breathtaking attractions when she finally opened the door for him.

"Good Lord!" Thack exhaled deeply, compulsively reaching out to touch her hair as he stepped into the room and closed and locked the door behind him.

The click of the lock springing into place caused a sense of unease to feather down Barbara's spine. "Wh—what's wrong?" she asked dryly, immediately swallowing to moisten her parched throat. The sudden lack of moisture in her mouth and throat had not been caused by the door being locked, but by the immediate response she felt to Thack's blatantly sensual appeal. Lord! Barbara thought weakly. Thack was positively, demoralizingly magnificent!

A tremor shivered through Barbara's body in unison with the heated gaze Thack sent on a slow journey from her still-damp hair to the tips of her bare toes. The arousal evident in the brown depths of his eyes sparked an answering arousal inside her mind and body. As Thack took one step forward, she took one step back.

"Thack, wait!" The hem of the cotton gown swirled around her ankles as she retreated hurriedly. "I—I—"

"Have cold feet?" Thack finished for her, a smile lifting the corners of his lips at the pun.

Barbara shook her head distractedly. "We—You, ah, you said we would talk!" A flash of panic speared through her as the back of her legs made contact with the end of the bed.

"And we will," Thack's smile promised endless delights. "Eventually," he added in a husky, pulse-stirring drawl.

Closing the distance between them, he lifted his hand to her hair, his expression one of wonder as he slid his fingers through the silken strands.

"So beautiful," he murmured, bending over her to bury his face in the mass of waves. "Why do you ever pull it into that knot at the top of your head?"

"Umm, ah, because it's so long and, ah-hem, so thick and—Oh!" Barbara gasped as Thack blew softly into her ear. "It, ah, gets so tangled if I let it free."

"I want your promise that you will always let it free for me," Thack murmured, moistening her ear with his warm breath.

"Thack!" Barbara moaned deeply. With the nearness of him, every uneasy sensation she'd experienced less than an hour ago was swamped by the surge of physical and emotional need.

What difference did it make how long she'd known him? Barbara wondered vaguely. She wanted him—all of him—his strength, his gentleness, his passion. Pushing her fears to the far edges of her consciousness, she lifted her face into his taut throat and pressed her lips to his warm, male-scented skin.

"Yes," Thack breathed, stroking his other hand down the length of her spine. "Oh, yes, honey, touch me, taste me—" his lips left a warm trail from her ear to her mouth "—then love me." Tangling his fingers in her hair, he held her still for his kiss.

If Barbara had considered Thack's earlier kisses arousing, she now learned how devastating his mouth

could be. The privacy of the room released all con-
straint and he parted her lips with his own, stroking the
sensitive flesh on the inside of her bottom lip with his
tongue before thrusting deeply into her mouth.

Whimpering a response, Barbara surrendered without a struggle. Coiling her arms around his neck, she
arched her body, instinctively seeking the source of his
heat.

Granting her silent plea, Thack slid his hand to the
base of her spine, splaying his long fingers as he urged
her into his hard readiness.

"Barbara. Barb. Honey." Thack groaned, raising his
head to stare into her passion-clouded eyes. "I love the
feel of my tongue inside your mouth, but it's not
enough. *I* want to be inside of you, my body filling
yours." Releasing her hair, he trailed his hand down the
side of her neck to her shoulders, then lower, inhaling
sharply at her shudder of response as his palm cupped
one small breast.

"I don't believe you have any more on under that
tentlike nightgown than I have under my clothes." A
satisfied smile feathered his lips.

He had come to her room fresh from the shower, his
wet hair the color of dark honey, his feet bare, his body
covered by a faded pair of jeans and a short-sleeved
shirt, the edges held loosely together by two buttons
fastened at his middle.

Barbara had suspected his nakedness under the two
pieces of clothing. *Knowing* that the only articles of attire separating their bodies were a shirt, jeans, and a
cotton nightgown fired her senses and imagination.

His touch light, Thack carefully drew the gown up
her body, gathering the folds in his broad hands before
slipping it over her head in one fluid motion. His fin-

gers were working on the shirt buttons before the gown
landed in a heap on the floor.

Shivering from the conflicting emotions of eager-
ness and trepidation, Barbara watched in unwilling
fascination as first the shirt then the jeans were tossed
on top of the gown.

In the natural state, Thack was excitingly intimidating. His tall, beautifully proportioned body was lean
and muscle-corded, and every inch of his skin was the
same golden bronze shade. Springy white-gold curls
clung to his broad chest, narrowing to a slender line
down his belly before circling around his manhood. His
long, straight legs were lightly dusted with finer, slightly
darker hair.

As Barbara's gaze drank in his male beauty, Thack's
dark eyes returned the compliment. When their glances
met they spoke simultaneously in the same hushed tone
of near awe.

"You're beautiful."

There was an instant of utter silence, then their mu-
tual laughter shattered the tension.

"Men aren't beautiful." Even as he murmured the
words, a pleased smile played over Thack's lips. Lifting his hand, he gently filled his fingers with a curling
lock of her hair, drawing it forward to rest against her
breast.

"You are," Barbara insisted, mesmerized by the
passion darkening his eyes.

Thack shook his head absently, too captivated by the
act of smoothing another lock of hair over her other
breast to respond aloud.

Beginning to tingle and ache for his touch, Barbara's
aroused nipples poked through the silken strands,
making an unmistakable demand for attention.

Thack's breathing growing noticeably uneven, he stared at the puckered points, then raised his eyes to tangle his smoky brown gaze with hers.

"I'm trembling!" Thack's hoarse voice held sheer incredulity. "Look at me." He lifted his hands for her to observe the tremor in his fingers. "I've never before actually trembled with need for a woman." He lowered his head slowly to her breast. "Let me love you, honey. I need to love you so much."

Barbara answered his plea by grasping his head to draw him to her. With the touch of his lips, then his tongue to her heated flesh, she speared her fingers into his damp hair, pressing, pressing urgently against his scalp with her fingertips while arching her back to give him access to her body.

Thack did not brush her hair to the side, but instead made love to her breasts through the fine silky strands. The sheer eroticism of his act weakened her knees and sparked a blaze in the heart of her desire. An incoherent murmur was wrenched from her tight throat with the first pull of his suckling lips. Had it not been for the strong arm he circled around her waist, Barbara would have crumpled to the floor at his feet.

As if aware of the heaviness weighing her limbs, Thack reluctantly relinquished his gentle grasp on the gem-hard nipple of her right breast. As he straightened, he swung her into his arms and strode to the side of the bed.

"This junk's got to go," he muttered, sweeping her packages onto the floor and then settling her on the bed.

There was a muted thunder in Barbara's ears, a drumming that kept time with the rapidity of her crazily pounding heart. Her skin felt prickly and overheated. Though leaden, her arms and legs felt restless.

She ached with a terrible emptiness. Automatically, she opened for him as he moved to join her on the bed.

Thack paused, a flicker of appreciative surprise flashing in his eyes, then he carefully slid his long body onto the bed and between her thighs. Propping himself on stiffened arms, he gazed tenderly into her eyes.

"Thank you," he whispered simply.

Barbara's eyes widened. "What for?" she asked in an unfamiliar, throaty voice.

"For wanting me as much as I want you."

Lowering his head, he took possession of her mouth. Sliding one hand under her, he lifted her as he took possession of her body. Coordinating the movement of his tongue and thrusting body, he initiated a rhythm older than time.

Within seconds Barbara's entire body was taut with tension. Her chest felt constricted. Above the slender ankles locked at the base of his spine, her toes curled in tight anticipation.

For the duration of a heartbeat, Thack broke the contact of their lips to drag air into his lungs, then his mouth captured hers again, and his tongue found the increased tempo.

Clinging to his back, Barbara stiffened from ever-tightening tension and then, for the first time in her life, she experienced the wild flight of release. His hands gripping her hips, Thack held her shuddering body tightly to him, absorbing her tremors with his body. When her harshly drawn breaths had subsided to mere gasps, he began to move again, faster and faster, thrusting ever deeper, as if in a desperate effort to become her, have her become him.

When the tension began to coil inside again, Barbara gasped for a different reason. Never with Peter had she found that pinnacle of ecstasy. Was she to thrill to it again, so soon?

Under her stroking palms and gripping thighs, Barbara felt Thack's muscles tightening. His chest expanded, crushing her to the bed. Barbara didn't care. Caught up in the spiraling tension, she strove toward the exploding ecstasy of perfect union. Thack tore his mouth from hers at their moment of achievement.

"Dear God, Barbara!" The strangled cry echoed in the room for an instant. Then his body collapsed onto hers.

Stunned by the experience, Barbara cradled his spent body tenderly to her breast, idly stroking his sweat-beaded hair as her breathing slowly returned to normal.

Did most women feel that fantastic soaring release at the end? she wondered, a smile of enchantment curving her lips. All these years, ever since high school, she'd heard of the flame that consumed the mind and body. She'd heard and hadn't believed. To encounter the proof of the claim now, as she approached her thirtieth year, was not unlike discovering there really was a Santa Claus after all!

Barbara compressed her lips to repress a chuckle. Feeling the silent laughter bubble inside her, Thack raised his head, a quizzical smile tilting his lips as he gazed down at her.

"My lovemaking's funny?" he asked teasingly, fully aware of her double completion, and not at all offended.

"Your lovemaking's the ultimate in perfection, and you know it." Barbara's smile teased back, as did the suggestive movement of her lower body, which continued to sheathe him.

Thack rewarded her play with a kiss that began sweetly but quickly proceeded to red hot. Tasting her lips, he was amazed at the spear of flame that flicked into his loins; his body hadn't regenerated this swiftly since he was a teenager!

Delighted with the sensation, himself, and Barbara, Thack deserted the honey of her mouth for the satin of her breasts. She was cream and sugar, as delicious as rich, dark chocolate. Curling his tongue around one taut peak, Thack shuddered to the thrill of expanding while still inside her warmth. At that moment he would have happily agreed to spend the remainder of his days thus connected to her. It was not to be. Spurred by the maddening sound of the soft noises Barbara was making deep in her throat, the tide of desire swept him out of control.

Incredibly, their attainment was again simultaneous.

This time, long minutes transpired before they came down from the heights. Thack was still breathing harshly when he levered his depleted body off of Barbara's. A smile softening his face, he drew her into his embrace, settling her head comfortably on his damp chest. He was quiet for so long Barbara was afraid he'd drifted into sleep.

"Thack?" she murmured, hopefully.

"Hmm?"

Barbara bit her lip. He'd said they would talk—but how to begin? Sliding her hand over his chest, she toyed with the swirls of springy hair.

"Tell me about your marriage," she blurted out timidly.

Thack sighed, but not repressively. "Talk time, huh?" A smile lurked in the tone of his low voice.

"Yes."

"I'm pretty dry," he drawled. "Can't imagine why." Tilting her head up by lifting her chin, he smiled into her eyes. "The wine's probably warm as—" He caught himself in time. "But it is wet." He contrived to look hopeful. "I talk one hell'u'va lot more when I'm sloshed, honey."

Laughing, Barbara pushed herself away from him. "Oh, get up and pour the wine, you big oaf!"

Laughing softly, Thack slid his fingers over her skin as she escaped his embrace. "Then again, maybe we don't need any further stimulant," he murmured, his gaze drifting over her.

"Thackery." Barbara managed to instill a warning note into her voice.

While mumbling, "You're no fun," he rolled to the side of the bed and stood up.

The room was bathed in a muted golden glow, cast from the almost horizontally slanted rays of the setting sun. Standing by the bed, Thack's sweat-glistened body was washed by the glory of dying sunlight.

Barbara gasped softly. The sight of his gold-bronze body highlighted by the sun's rays was stunning. But that was not what wrenched the sharp breath from her throat.

"Oh, Thack!" Barbara breathed achingly, her shocked gaze clinging to the fine white lines scarring the perfection of his back. "Is that what the barbed wire did to your back?"

Supremely unselfconscious about his nudity, Thack turned to face her, a tender smile curving his lips. The smile faded as he glimpsed her horrified expression.

"Don't look like that, honey!" Propping his right knee on the bed, he leaned across it to her. "It happened a long time ago. All that's left are the marks."

"But your beautiful back!" she moaned, biting her lip as she gazed up at him, the expression in her hazel eyes eloquent.

"Oh, Lord." Ensnared within her anguished gaze, Thack felt himself sinking for the third time. He was a goner, sure as thunder follows lightning. "Sweet love, don't." Lifting his hand, he stroked her cheek, eyes widening as his fingers were wet by her tears. She was crying! Dear God! Barbara was crying for him, crying for wounds he'd received more than ten years ago!

Thack felt like he was shattering into tiny fragments inside. His throat tightened painfully as he carefully worked his injured leg onto the bed to sit facing her.

"Barb?" There was a hoarse, husky tone in his voice that Thack had never heard before. As if stroking delicate china, he brushed the tears from her cheeks. No one, no woman had ever cried for him—not even his wife, and she'd been there at the hospital when the wounds were treated! "Darling, why are you crying?" Merely speaking hurt his throat.

"Oh, Thack, I'm being silly, I know." Barbara's tears washed his fingertips. "But...I feel it...the pain." She drew a ragged breath. "Not on the skin on the outside of my back, but inside—deep, deep inside." Her eyes were wide with wonder and confusion.

"I should have been there for you!"

Her anguished cry sent a shaft of pain into Thack's chest. *I should have been there for you.* The echo of her cry reverberated in his mind. Tremors shivering over his body, he stared at her, his dark eyes glowing. No one had *ever* been there for him—not mother, father, wife or lover—no one! And now, this woman, this uptight, high-class, New York model—this thoroughly beautiful person—was suffering over something that had happened to him years before she'd ever heard of him!

Thack closed his eyes against the burning sting of hot moisture that filled them. Drawing her trembling body into his arms, he held her tightly, moving slowly back and forth, uncertain and not caring if the gentle rocking was to soothe Barbara or to comfort himself. His arms tightened convulsively as a tremor quaked through his long torso.

"Oh, honey." Thack nuzzled his face into her scented hair. "Do you have any idea what you're doing to me?"

"No. What?" Barbara sniffled.

Completely enthralled, Thack didn't hesitate. "Ripping me apart inside." He tightened the embrace when her body jerked in reaction. "Do you have any idea how long and hard I worked to achieve this carefree attitude?"

Intrigued, Barbara angled her head to gaze up at him. "Attitude?" she repeated softly. "What do you mean?"

Unshed tears had brightened his dark eyes. The removal of the barriers he'd erected revealed the naked hunger and longing in the softened brown depths of his eyes.

"I think it's talk time, honey." His lips curved in a heartrendingly uncertain smile. "That is, if you really want to hear it?"

"But of course I want to hear it!" Barbara exclaimed immediately. A fresh rush of tears blurred her vision as a shuddering sigh of relief whispered through his taut lips. What sort of life has this man had? she wondered, hurting for him.

"Okay." His movements unnaturally awkward, Thack backed off the bed. "Ah, well, where should I start?'' Obviously restless, he prowled around the now almost dark room.

"Wherever you like," Barbara responded, straining to see him.

Thack came to a dead stop at the foot of the bed. "Yeah...um, I think I'll pour us some wine first." Moving again, he found the switch on the floor lamp, illuminating the room with a dim glow from the single low-watt bulb.

Everything about his actions shouted of his vulnerability. A gentle smile playing on her lips, Barbara slid off her side of the bed to place a hand on his arm. "I'll understand if you'd rather forget it." Her tone was deep with reassurance.

"No." Thack's big hand swallowed hers. "I just might be a little slow getting started. I've never done the confessional bit to anyone."

"But you want to with me?" Barbara shivered as she realized the extent of the trust he was placing in her.

"Yes." Again Thack's answer came unhesitatingly.

"All right." Bending, she scooped up the cotton gown. "I'll freshen up while you pour the wine." Spinning away, she headed for the bathroom. Thack's voice stopped her at the doorway.

"You're not going to put on that tent, are you?" he asked plaintively.

Barbara tossed him an arched look over her shoulder. "Nakedness is not conducive to conversation," she said repressively.

Thack groaned. "I suppose that means you'd like me to put on my jeans?"

"I'd appreciate it." Barbara's eyes sparked with mischief. "Otherwise, you'll have a very unsettling effect on my libido."

Thack took a step toward her and with a soft yelp, Barbara dashed into the relative safety of the bathroom.

A few minutes later, refreshed by a quick sponge bath, her slender body concealed by the flowing folds of the cotton nightgown, Barbara sat cross-legged on the bed facing the headboard and the jean-clad man propped against it.

Sipping at the warm wine Thack had poured into a plastic glass provided by the motel, she invited softly, "In your own time, in your own way, Thack."

Nine

"There's a man walking around somewhere in northern California wearing my face."

For a moment, Barbara stared at Thack in stunned confusion, then the meaning of what he'd said hit her. "You have a twin?" Incredulity laced her tone.

Thack nodded his head. "Yep, identical." He frowned. "At least we *were* identical as babies. I haven't the vaguest idea what he looks like now." A cynical smile twisted his lips. "I haven't seen him since I was five."

"You were separated when you were five years old?" Barbara asked in disbelief.

"That's correct." Thack's shoulders lifted in an unconvincing shrug. "My parents thought it was the fair thing to do when they divorced."

"Fair?" Barbara repeated softly, then in a screech, "Fair!"

"Cute, huh?" Thack's drawl was as unconvincing as his shrug. "You'd have to understand my mother." His lips twisted again. "I think she had an air tunnel between her ears. She was a genuine fluff brain. She was also a Southern belle. My father met her while he was attending a pharmaceutical convention in New Orleans."

"Your father was a pharmacist?" Barbara asked, thoroughly confused.

"Yes. He owned a drugstore in Fort Stockton." Thack's lips quirked appealingly. "You envisioned a rancher?"

"Well, yes," Barbara smiled. "I guess so."

Thack shook his head. "Not my father. He didn't like getting his hands dirty. Now my grandfather," Thack smiled with remembrance. "*He* was a rancher. I inherited my spread from him."

"You loved him," Barbara stated quietly, definitely.

"Very much." Thack finished the wine in his glass and refilled it at once. "He raised me until his death, when I was fourteen. Then I went back to my father."

"And your brother?" Barbara asked gently.

"He was raised in California, by my mother and her second husband."

Barbara ached for the devastated little boy hiding inside the tall, capable man. "Why did your parents divorce?" she probed softly.

"Probably because they never should have married in the first place." Thack snorted. "Hell! They only knew each other three days! Three lousy days! How can you build a lifetime on that?" he demanded.

She hesitated to remind him that *they* were in a motel room together and had known each other for exactly the same amount of time. But then, Thack hadn't mentioned anything about a lifetime together, either. She concealed a sigh behind her glass.

"Anyway," he continued when she made no response. "They got married in New Orleans and he brought her back to Texas. And she hated it with a passion." Thack shrugged. "By the time I was five, the hatred outweighed whatever love she'd ever felt for my father. She took my brother and ran to California; I was left with a very bitter father. He died hating . . . everything."

"What's your brother's name?" Barbara asked, attempting to draw him from the memory of his father.

A teasing smile tilted the corners of Thack's lips. "Are you ready?" He arched one brow at her. Barbara nodded, frowning. "Zackery," he said distinctly.

Barbara burst out laughing. "You're putting me on!" she choked. "Thackery and Zackery!"

"I told you my mother was a fluff brain," Thack laughed with her.

"I know, but, honestly, Thack and Zack! It's absolutely too precious!"

"Yeah," Thack agreed. "Maybe it's best we weren't raised together." He didn't really believe that, and Barbara knew it. Still, she kept silent, and after a moment he continued. "I keep telling myself that I'll go to the coast and look him up some day."

"And will you?"

"Hell knows." Thack grimaced. "You still want to hear about my wife?"

Change of subject, Barbara thought, achingly. "Only if you want to tell me about her," she replied.

Sipping at his wine, his eyes glittered at her over the rim of the plastic glass. "I'd rather make love with you again," he murmured. "But, I might as well get it the hell over with."

Having kept a running score of the number of times he'd cursed, Barbara narrowed her eyes and deliberately reached for her purse on the floor beside the bed. Calmly removing her cigarettes from the bag, she extracted one and lit up, silently daring him to object. He frowned, but prudently kept his mouth shut.

"I met Alice, my wife, while I was attending the police academy," he began. Barbara interrupted.

"You've had professional training?"

Thack contrived to look insulted. "I'll have you know, you are dealing with a fully trained law enforcement officer here. Now, if you want to hear this boring story, shut up and listen."

"Yes, Mr. Officer, sir." Barbara lowered her eyes meekly... and puffed rapidly on her cigarette.

Laughing softly, Thack leaned to her to raise her head with his hand. "Put that thing out and come sit beside me," he coaxed. "I'm lonely."

Barbara didn't require coaxing. Slipping from the bed she crushed the cigarette out in the ashtray, then settled down close to him with a murmured, "Continue, please. I'll be quiet."

"Alice was tiny, delicate, and cotton-candy sweet." As he resumed his tale, Thack shifted to face her. "She was also very self-sufficient and independent." His shoulders rippled in a shrug. "I had no problem with that. In fact, I was flattered by her interest in me." His lips twisted wryly. "I toppled like a felled tree."

"You loved her?" Already disliking the woman intensely, Barbara found it difficult to ask the question.

"Madly," Thack drawled sardonically, smiling into her narrowed eyes. "I was very young, very inexperienced, and very horny." He laughed with delight as she flushed.

"You still are—the latter, I mean," Barbara retaliated.

"This is true," Thack agreed solemnly, his eyes gleaming with inner amusement.

Barbara's lips twitched with a reluctant smile. "Get on with it, Sharp!"

Thack laughed aloud. "Anyway," he waved one hand aimlessly. "Alice owned an exclusive boutique, had big plans, and even bigger ambitions." He sighed. "Things were okay for a couple'a years, then her business expanded and I got restless."

He got restless? Barbara felt a pang of unease. For all his earlier talk about fidelity, was Thack the kind of man who was quickly bored with any woman? "Restless?" she probed fearfully.

"Yeah." Thack shook his head ruefully. "For as much as I loved law enforcement, I hated wearing the uniform, and didn't like the confinement of the patrol car and the regimentation. When I told Alice that I wanted to join the Rangers, she said, 'Fine, I'll see you around,' and that was the end of it."

Not likely. Barbara didn't voice the thought. Though Thack was smiling, the smile didn't banish the shadow of pain from his eyes. "And the only person you have is a brother you haven't seen in all these years?" she asked gently.

"That's about it. Just like the only person you have is Aunt Ellie."

"Aunt Ellie!" Barbara screeched, bolting upright. "I must call her, tell her where I am!"

Thack's arm clasped her firmly to his side. "Relax, honey. I called her before I had my shower. She knows where you are, and that you're safe."

Safe? Barbara swallowed a burst of nervous laughter. She was in a motel room in a very compromising position on a bed with the most complex man she'd ever met. Safe? Thackery Sharp was positively lethal—and extremely dangerous to her emotional health! Beneath the easygoing, laid-back facade he assumed, Thack was one hell'u'va man. At that instant, Barbara realized that she would very likely love Thack until the day she died. The realization scared the wits out of her. Barbara was drawn from her thoughts by Thack's fingers tugging on her gown.

"Ah, honey," he murmured when she looked up at him. "Do you think I could talk you out of that tent?"

Electrical tension sizzled through her body. Automatically, her fingers groped for the cigarette pack. His broad hand covered hers.

"The tradition is to have a smoke *after* the act," he teased.

Barbara blurted the first thing that came into her mind. "Are you repelled by the taste of smoke on my mouth?"

"On the contrary," he smiled. To prove his point, Thack bent his head to kiss her, deeply.

The cigarette pack fell to the floor. Her breathing was suddenly uneven. "Ah, why did you quit?" Barbara wondered aloud, her body beginning to tremble from the touch of his wandering hands.

"Not for the usual reasons," he replied distractedly, testing the tip of one breast with the tip of one finger. A slow smile curved his lips when she shivered in response. "When I realized I was up to two packs a day,

I decided to run an experiment." Very casually he began to draw the gown up the length of her body.

Barbara lifted her hips absently. "What, ah, sort of experiment?" She moaned in response to the caressing glide of his palms. Then the gown flew into a corner, and she trembled violently under the heat of his gaze.

"I wanted to discover which one of us was stronger," Thack muttered, grunting as he shucked the jeans from his long legs. "Me or the weed." Reaching for her, he slid them both down, flat on the mattress. "So far, I've kept the upper hand." His parted lips teased hers, his need pressed urgently against her thigh.

"And . . . and the chocolate?" Barbara could barely breathe, or keep her restless legs still.

"You know about that, too?" He laughed softly, filling her mouth with his warm breath. "The chocolate's a different thing. Eating chocolate is very sensual. Second only to making love."

Vaguely, Barbara realized that she would never again be able to look at chocolate without making the sexy connection. Then all lucid thought was wiped from her mind by the gentle probe of his tongue.

For long minutes Barbara was lost to everything but the excitement created by Thack's hands and mouth as he searched out and discovered every sensitive spot on her body. Responding to the sensual stimuli, she reciprocated, stroking his arms, shoulders, back and chest, and then, bravely, his hips and taut flanks. Then, fascinated by the shiver she wrenched from him by trailing her fingers up his thighs, she abandoned caution and took him into her soft hands.

"Oh, God, honey, yes," Thack groaned harshly, settling his length between her thighs. "Bring me to you!"

Eagerly obeying his pleading command, she guided his passage, gasping with pleasure as he thrust urgently into her body. When he went still for a moment, closing his eyes as he savored the thrill of being sheathed by her velvet moistness, she voiced the hope hovering at the back of her mind.

"Will it happen again, Thack?" His eyes opened as he frowned uncomprehendingly at her. "I mean, that feeling of explosion, that shattering into a million sparkling pieces?"

Shock widened his passion-darkened eyes. "Do you mean that that was the first time you'd ever experienced . . . ah . . . full completion?" he asked in a tone of awed astonishment.

Barbara's cheeks were warm with embarrassment. "Yes," she admitted huskily. "It was . . . wonderful," she added honestly.

"And it will be again," Thack promised, beginning to move his body in a mesmerizing rhythm.

And it was, not once, but three times more before he allowed her to drift into blissful slumber.

It was raining! Lifting her face to absorb the gentle fall of reviving moisture, Barbara let her gaze skim the rugged mountains whose peaks were shrouded by clouds. It was early afternoon, and she and Thack had been in the Big Bend park since right after daybreak.

Lowering her head, she stared in awe at the sheer canyon walls that rose majestically from the Rio Grande far below.

"Impressed?" Thack asked from beside her, curling a strong arm around her waist.

"Very," she admitted, moving a hand to indicate not only the canyon, but the entire area. "Words are hardly adequate to describe the majesty of it all." She raised her gaze to the verdant green mountains.

"It isn't always like this," Thack murmured, moving to stand behind her. "Every decade or so, the Big Bend is treated to long summer rains instead of the on-and-off-again storm. And, when it is, the mountains turn green, the grasses grow tall, and there's an abundance of brilliant wildflowers—" he chuckled "—just like the ones you've been raving about all morning."

Barbara didn't protest his teasing. She couldn't, for she *had* been raving all morning, enthralled by the wildly primitive beauty of the park from the moment they'd entered the Basin campground.

While in the campground, Barbara had wandered around curiously, peeking in at the Chisos Mountain lodge, which catered to overnight guests, and checking out the Chisos Remuda, where tourists could arrange for saddle horses, pack animals and guides. Thack had conferred with park rangers while she poked around. When he'd caught up with her, on her way to the establishment offering groceries, camping supplies and such, he was wearing a self-satisfied smile.

"I judge the rangers could help you?" Barbara lifted her brows questioningly as he steered her back to the pickup.

Thack nodded. "It took some time, but the information came in. Our three thieves were observed near Terlingua Abaja last night. They were setting up camp." His smile grew wolfish. "The reason the ranger noticed them was because one of the men was obviously injured."

"Terlingua?" Barbara repeated. "Do you mean we have to go back to the ghost town?"

"No. Terlingua Abaja is a primitive campsite along the Terlingua Creek, down near Santa Elena Canyon." He'd helped her into the truck. "It'll take us a while to get there, and at times the going will be a little rough, so hang on, honey."

Now, Barbara smiled wryly at Thack's earlier understatement. A little rough barely covered the jolting ride. He'd made this stop as a silent apology for the rough trip and to give her the opportunity to look out over the canyon.

Grateful for the respite, whatever the reason, Barbara sighed and rested her head against his flatly muscled chest. A shiver snaked down her spine as his hand slowly glided up her rib cage then covered her breast possessively.

"Who was he?" Thack murmured into her hair.

Bemused by the grandeur of the scenery surrounding her, Barbara frowned in confusion. "Who was who?"

Thack's fingers flexed into her soft flesh. "The man who was unable to give you those shattering explosions." He rubbed his face in the mane she'd let flow free at his request. "The man you mentioned while we were in Terlingua."

Barbara raked her memory. She knew of course. She had told Thack there had only ever been one man. "His name is Peter Vanzant."

"Your friend Nicole's rich, powerful brother." Thack's fingers dug into her tender breast, then eased when she gasped. "I'm sorry," he muttered. "Tell me about him."

Barbara didn't hesitate. Thack had opened himself to her; she couldn't offer him less. Her voice devoid of inflection, she recounted her affair with Peter, leaving nothing out.

"Were you in love with him?" Thack's flat tone mirrored hers.

"Yes."

"And yet you left him." A fine edge appeared to roughen his voice.

"Yes." Barbara shivered. What was he thinking?

"I'm damned glad you did." Thack didn't attempt to conceal the relief he felt. "And there's been no one else?"

Barbara overlooked the curse—his first of the day. "No one." The sincerity in her voice left no room for doubt. "Till now," she whispered, closing her eyes with pleasure as his hand caressed her breast.

"God, I want you!" Thack growled, seeking the curve of her neck with his hungry lips. "And I've got to go chasing around this wilderness hunting three lousy yo-yos!" Releasing her, he stepped back abruptly. "Let's go, honey." Grasping her hand, he strode to the truck. "Before you find yourself being seduced on the edge of a canyon."

The prospect had its appeal. Smiling secretly, Barbara allowed herself to be bundled into the pickup. Musing on what it might feel like to make love in the open with the fine rain washing their heated bodies, she absently reached for a cigarette—*her* first of the day.

As he had the night before, Thack stopped her by placing his hand over hers. "Do you really need it?" he asked gently.

Barbara's eyes widened as she considered the question. Incredibly, she realized that she really didn't need the smoke! A startled gurgle of laughter burst from her throat.

"No, I don't need it!" She hefted the pack in her hand a moment, then tossed it aside. "You're more than enough stimulant for me!"

Thack's low, sexy laughter sent a quiver all the way down to the toes inside her stout walking shoes. "And I'll prove it to you," he promised, slanting a meaningful glance at her. "Just as soon as I round up our inept gold thieves and pack them off to the authorities."

His mention of the thieves chilled Barbara. "Are these men inept, Thack?" she asked hopefully.

"In spades," he declared convincingly. "Their actions prove it. If they'd known what they were doing, they'd have been long gone by now. So, where are these clowns?" He snorted. "Hanging out in the hills that are overrun with tourists and park rangers." He shook his head in disgust. "Hell, this isn't a manhunt. It's a damn fish-barrel shoot."

"You swear one more time, Thackery Sharp, and *I* swear I'll get out those cigarettes!" Barbara warned softly.

"Oh, Barb!" Thack shot her a pained look. "Hell and damn aren't actually swearing, are they?" His lips twitched. "Now *real* swearing is an art. Do you want to hear some of the more colorful curses in my repertoire?"

"I think I'll pass, thank you." Barbara managed to look prim, earning herself a bark of delighted laughter from Thack. Deciding to quit while she at least *thought* she was ahead, she subsided with a superior smile.

Beside her, Thack was also quiet, tormented by Barbara's narrative.

She had left him. Knowing she loved Peter Vanzant, Barbara had coolly walked away from him and the luxury love nest he'd provided for her. Would she as coolly walk away from a disillusioned Texas Ranger? The mere thought of losing her now incited an emotion akin to terror in Thack.

Expertly steering the pickup over the rough road, Thack examined his feelings and immediately diagnosed his condition as incurable love. Thack couldn't decide whether to whoop like a wild Indian or bawl like a lost heifer. He did neither. Instead, he slanted a quick glance at Barbara. Lord, she was lovely!

The pickup lurched to the side as the right front tire climbed over a small rock. Thack cursed to himself. Keep your mind on the business at hand, you idiot! Take care of personal business later.

But, damn! Barbara did look tasty decked out in the blue jeans, plaid shirt and denim jacket he'd insisted on paying for at the dry goods store—not at all like a New York model who could demand a small mint for a day's work.

Clamping his lips against a sigh, Thack concentrated on his driving, and wished for a large box of chocolates.

What is he thinking? Barbara wondered, watching his lips flatten into a straight, forbidding line. Perhaps he was gearing himself mentally for what lay ahead. What *did* lie ahead? Barbara repressed a sigh of apprehension.

Her uneasiness was not caused by the fear of what they might find at the place called Terlingua Abaja, but what might occur after their crazy manhunt was over.

That she was deeply in love with Thack, Barbara now accepted as fact. She was also positive that, this time, her love would endure the test of time; there would be no freedom from the pangs of the emotion after a period of eighteen months. No, Barbara sadly suspected that with Thack, she was in for the long haul.

From beneath lowered lashes, she swept a loving glance over his appealing form. Lord, he was handsome! Too handsome for her good. He was dressed in much the same manner as on the day she'd first seen him: tan shirt, trousers, boots and Stetson. The single difference in clothing was the addition of a dark brown suede vest. With his coloring and clothing, Thack blended in with the terrain she'd seen. Barbara was certain Thack's choice of attire was part and parcel of his occupation.

A lawman. Barbara fought the tremor that shivered over her skin. Her aunt's recitation of Thack's accumulated injuries whispered in her mind. How did a woman learn to live with a man who seemed hell-bent on doing himself bodily injury?

The speculation brought Barbara up straight. Live with Thack? Where had that idea come from? Barbara's gaze caressed his finely chiseled, sternly set face. She forced her glance forward when her eyes began to sting. Dear heaven, she thought achingly, she would gladly give anything for the opportunity to live with Thack and, possibly, erase the years of pain and rejection concealed behind that wall of laid-back carelessness.

"We're here." Thack brought the pickup to a stop as he spoke.

As quiet as his voice was, Barbara jerked as if he'd shouted at her.

"Are you afraid?" Without waiting for her to reply, he decided, "I think you'd better wait in the truck."

"No!" Barbara protested sharply. There was no way she was going to allow him to go out there alone, and possibly get himself hurt again. "I'm not afraid," she denied bravely, glancing around the desolate area nervously. "At least, not *too* afraid."

"Barb—" Thack sounded like he might argue; Barbara didn't give him the chance.

"I'd be a nervous wreck waiting here alone." Pushing the door open, she jumped to the ground.

The light rainfall had stopped, but misty clouds still clung like angel hair to the mountains. Ignoring Thack's mutter as he stepped from the pickup, Barbara glanced around, slightly amazed to discover that she was really beginning to appreciate the harsh beauty of the unfriendly land.

"That little spurt of rain helped us," Thack remarked, carefully closing the door.

Glancing around to face him, Barbara inhaled roughly as her gaze registered the rifle in his right hand and the holstered pistol belted around his narrow waist. Good grief! she wondered wildly, what have I let myself in for here?

Positive Thack would order her to wait in the truck if she revealed a hint of fear, she attempted to act cool.

"Ah... going to war, Thack?" Playing the sophisticate, she arched one eyebrow, indicating the weaponry with a casual wave of her hand.

"If necessary." Thack's calm tone warned that he wasn't attempting anything; he was being exactly what he was—a trained lawman. "Second thoughts?" One white-gold brow mimicked hers.

"No, of course not," Barbara said swiftly, too swiftly. "In, ah, what way has the rain helped?" She decided a change of subject was called for, and sighed when, with a tiny, knowing smile, Thack indicated the ground with the rifle.

"It made everything damp enough to take the imprint of tire tracks, but not wet enough to wash them away."

"The thieves are here then?" Somehow, Barbara managed to keep her voice steady.

Thack didn't look up from his examination of the terrain. "Someone's here," he murmured, slowly moving to follow the tracks. "Stay behind me, honey," he cautioned when she started to walk beside him. "A good distance behind me."

Trailing a few feet behind Thack, Barbara shuddered inside the denim jacket despite the growing heat now that the rain had ceased. There was an almost unnatural silence about the place that was chilling.

Did the ghosts of the ancients prowl these rugged mountain ranges and deserts? Did they lie in wait for the despoilers of this harshly beautiful section of West Texas?

Blinking, Barbara tried to curb her fanciful thoughts. She told herself that she was frightened enough by what might lie ahead without scaring herself witless by imagining ancient ghosts as well. Shaking herself out of the mood, she kept her gaze glued to Thack's reassuringly broad shoulders and back.

When he suddenly reached back to stop her, Barbara had to bite on her lip to muffle a startled yelp. A huge boulder some fifteen or twenty feet in front of them barred their path. Using hand motions, Thack indicated the boulder, then himself, then, quite effectively, silently told her to stay put. Before she could even think of protesting he was soundlessly moving away from her.

There ensued an almost eerie quiet. After what Barbara felt positive had to be an hour, or at least ten minutes, Thack called to her.

"Barb. I need help."

Was Thack hurt—again? Muffling a cry, she took off at a stumbling run, concern for him making her completly unconcerned for her own safety.

"Whoa, hold it!" Thack halted her precipitous dash around the boulder with the sharp command. "Easy, honey," he went on softly. "I don't want you stepping into the line of fire."

Line of fire! Barbara came to a jarring stop, eyes widening at the scene before her. Thack was standing with his back to the boulder, rifle at the ready against his shoulder. The battered truck Barbara remembered vividly from the day before was parked approximately ten or fifteen yards beyond him. A crude camp had been set up in front of the truck. The two men in evidence, one lying on a sleeping bag, the other down on his haunches, were frozen into position, warily eyeing the man with the rifle.

"Now, honey," Thack spoke very softly, for her ears alone. "What I want you to do is circle around those two bandits," he instructed, his gaze riveted to the rifle sight. "When you're behind them, I want you to very carefully relieve them of their weapons," he continued quietly. Then his tone hardened. "Not at any time are you to move between me and them. Is that clear?"

"Y-yes, Thack." Even as she was answering him, Barbara was asking herself what she was doing there. The question was academic; she *was* there and, strangely, obviously prepared to do whatever Thack asked of her, for she was already moving to obey.

"Slowly, honey," he advised, his voice oddly tight sounding.

Following his instructions, Barbara made a wide berth around the two silent men, coming up behind them as delicately as if the damp, sandy ground were covered with ice.

There were five weapons in all—three rifles, which she removed from the rack mounted on the back of the truck's cab, and two handguns, which she cautiously retrieved from the ground near the two men.

Beginning to breathe a little easier, Barbara clutched the weapons in her arms, then carefully retraced her steps back to the far side of the boulder. As far as she could tell, Thack had not moved as much as a muscle while she carried out his orders.

"Very good," he approved in that same low tone as she knelt to place the guns on the ground,.

Pleasurable warmth surged through her, heating her cheeks with color. Lord, she must really be besotted with the man, Barbara reflected wonderingly, if the mildest praise from him could affect her so strongly. A pleased smile tilting her lips, she began to rise, then froze at the sound of a harsh, yet clearly nervous voice that sounded from the other side of the boulder.

"If you want to go on breathin', tall man, you'll put down that rifle...slow and easy."

Ten

For one shocked instant Barbara was frozen in suspended motion. Her gaze registered the slight ripple as Thack's muscles tautened. The realization of the demand hit her; whoever it was, the man had addressed the command to Thack alone.

Coming out of her near trance, Barbara swiftly added one and one and came up with two. Two against one, in fact. If she couldn't see him, didn't it follow that he probably could not see her?

Still in a crouch, Barbara began moving stealthily around the back of the boulder. She had just about gotten around it when she remembered the weapons she'd placed so carefully on the ground. Oh, well, she sighed fatalistically, she hadn't the vaguest idea how to handle a gun anyway.

But she did know how to use her hands and feet. Thanking the urge that had sent her to self-defense classes several years before, Barbara inched around the rock until she had the man in view.

He was not very tall, a little chunky, and his features were rigid with strain. A pudgy hand gripped the pearl handle of a nasty-looking handgun. Peripherally, she noted Thack's motion as he was bending from the waist to lay the rifle on the ground.

Barbara drew a long, slow, calming breath. Then, with a short sharp cry vibrating from her throat, she went into action. Raising her arms into the defensive position, she leaped from behind the boulder onto the ground between Thack and the gunman.

"Hey!" The startled gunman exclaimed.

"What the—" Thack began.

Within seconds it was over. Her movements faster than the eye could follow, Barbara leaped into a scissor kick, her long right leg flashing out. The pistol was jerked from the man's hands by the impact of her toe at the moment the stiffened edge of her hand chopped into the side of his neck. The gunman dropped to the ground without a sound.

Hot damn! If you let this one get away from you ol' son, you are absolutely crazy. This is some kind of woman!

His thoughts still a trifle rattled, Thack sliced a quick glance at the woman curled up on the seat next to him, using his shoulder for a pillow.

Barbara had succumbed to sleep less than an hour after they'd finally driven out of the Big Bend park's environs. That had been hours ago; they would shortly arrive at the Holcomb ranch.

Thack had spent every one of those hours marveling over the climactic events of their manhunt. After Barbara's swift intervention into the play, the mop-up had seemed pretty dull by comparison.

Thack had tied the thieves up with rope he'd found in their truck. The rope hadn't been the only thing he'd found. Aside from a pile of canvas-covered supplies, which he felt sure had been stolen from the town of Tortilla, he had discovered Ellie's gold hidden under the seat in the cab of the dilapidated vehicle.

After stashing the gold in his pickup, Thack had contacted the park rangers on his CB. The rangers had arrived on the scene to offer assistance with the criminals, then they'd all made their way back to the Basin campground. To Thack, it had all been pretty routine and boring.

With a promise to bring Ellie into Sanderson to identify the thieves, he'd left them in the rangers' capable hands to await the arrival of the authorities, and had driven away with a very tired New York model.

But, holy night! The model *was* something else! A soundless laugh moved Thack's chest as the echo of her explanation drifted into his mind.

Thack had actually gawked at her, open-mouthed, after she'd rendered the gunman unconscious. Not entirely witless, he'd whipped his own rifle from the ground, training it on the other two thieves as he breathed, "Where in hell did you learn that?"

"I took lessons. I live in New York City, remember?"

With that, she had left the rest in Thack's capable hands. She had sat down on the ground, burying her face in the arms she clasped around her up-drawn knees. She'd refused to even look at the thieves again.

The ripple of soft laughter woke Barbara. Frowning, she angled her head to gaze up at Thack.

"Have you finally slipped over the edge?" she murmured sleepily, smiling despite her confusion.

"No, honey, I haven't slipped over the edge." Thack shot an amused glance at her. "I'm still enjoying the memory of your little demonstration of self-defense." His face sobered. "You were pretty terrific, you know."

"Or pretty stupid," she countered, flushing with pleasure at his praise. Moving swiftly, she straightened on the seat. "Where are we?" she asked as she yawned, deliberately changing the subject.

"Almost home." Thack waved his fingers at the windshield. "There's the sign for your aunt's property."

Almost home. Barbara felt her spirits plummet. What would happen now? Would Thackery Sharp ride off into the sunset like the mythical heroes of her youth? Barbara wondered, watching her aunt hobble onto the porch as Thack brought the pickup to a stop. Out of the corner of her eye, she saw J.B. approach the truck from the side of the house. Sighing, she pushed the door open. As she jumped to the dusty ground a depressing thought occurred to her.

A one-night stand in a motel is hardly a commitment.

In the ensuing confusion of hugs, greetings and the demand for explanations, Barbara didn't notice that Thack remained seated in the pickup. But J.B. did.

"You headed back to town?" J.B. inquired in that beautiful low voice of his.

Barbara glanced around in time to see Thack nod. "I've got to report to the sheriff's office," he explained. "And get cleaned up." He indicated his clothes with a motion of his hand. "I'll be back in the morning." His gaze drilled into Barbara. "Early in the morning."

"But what about my gold?" Ellie demanded.

And what about me? Barbara wailed silently.

"I'm going to sleep with it, then deposit it in the bank for you," Thack replied, shifting his gaze to Ellie. "I'll bring you a receipt in the morning." Without another word, he turned the pickup around and drove away.

As had happened a few mornings previously, Barbara was wakened by the light rap of knuckles on her bedroom door. Remembering the incident, and who had been knocking, her heart kicked into high gear.

"Phone for you, Barbara." The pleasing sound of J.B.'s voice shot down her soaring hopes. "It's New York again."

Barbara reached for her robe while stumbling from the bed. What could her agent want at this time of the morning? she grumbled, forgetting the time difference between New York and Texas. Come to that, she mused, what had Dan wanted when he called the day before?

Barbara, Ellie and J.B. had sat at the kitchen table, drinking coffee and talking until long into the early morning hours. It was not until Barbara had retired that her aunt remembered to tell her that Dan had called.

"Hello," Barbara muttered into the receiver. Her drooping eyes flew open at the charge of energy that her agent transmitted over the miles of telephone cables.

"Where the devil have you been?" Dan demanded, then charged on before she could answer. "No, never mind. Babsy, get on the first plane available. I've got a big one for you—a real dream of an assignment!"

"Dan, slow down! What are you talking about?" Barbara was fully awake now, awake and concerned. Where was Thack? Dan broke in on the thought as it formed.

"I'm talking about that series of commercials for the Satin Skin cosmetics company," Dan yelled excitedly. "It's yours, babe. But you've got to get back here at once!"

Satin Skin. Lord! Dan wasn't all excited for nothing. Satin Skin was about as big as the assignments came! But where was Thack? Barbara skimmed her gaze over the empty ranch yard. He had said he'd be early.

"Bar-bar-a," Dan wailed. "Are you in shock?"

No, Dan, I'm in love. Barbara didn't speak the thought aloud. "No, Dan, I'm thinking," she responded softly.

"Do me a favor, Babsy," Dan retorted. "Don't stand around wasting time thinking. Get hustling. I need you back here."

What should she do? Barbara bit her lip. Suddenly, the plum assignment, and the money and recognition that went with it were meaningless to her. The familiar spires of Manhattan were alien. And this desolate, dry, relentless and beautiful part of Texas was home, simply because Thack was here.

But she owed this to Dan for all the years he'd faithfully, and tirelessly worked to further her career. And, perhaps she owed it to herself as well. A smile curved her soft lips. It would be nice to retire in triumph. Not for a second did she allow herself to consider the possibility that Thack wouldn't want her. He *had* to want her—if he didn't she'd just die.

"OKay, Dan, I'll be there as soon as I can arrange it." Replacing the receiver, Barbara told herself that New York would be soon enough to tell Dan of her decision to quit modeling.

Barbara was fully dressed and brushing her hair when once again there was a gentle rap on her door. This time the voice that filtered through the wood panels was the only one in the world she wanted to hear.

"Barb, may I come in?" Thack asked softly.

"Yes." Barbara carefully placed the brush on the dresser surface, then slowly turned to face the man who had become her entire universe. "Good morning," she greeted him in a whisper.

"Good morning." The smile that curved his lips was so very tender it brought the sting of tears to her eyes. Crossing to her in a few long-legged strides, Thack pulled her into his arms and crushed her mouth with his. "Lord, I was hungry for you," he murmured as he raised his head to gaze into her eyes. "Did you miss me?" His tone held that hint of uncertainty she'd heard two days before, when he'd asked her if she liked him.

"Something terrible," Barbara admitted frankly.

Thack's smile grew breathtaking. "You can't imagine how relieved I am to hear you say that." His tone took on a jubilant note. Dipping his fingers into his back jeans pocket, he retrieved a folded business envelope. "Do you know what this is?" he asked, waving it in front of her.

Aware the question was a rhetorical one, Barbara shook her head.

"*This* is a letter from a San Francisco law firm informing me that I have been named as one of the beneficiaries of my mother's estate."

Shock widened Barbara's eyes. "Your mother died?"

The animation went out of Thack's face and his eyes darkened. "Yes." He gazed at her steadily. "I can't pretend sorrow, Barb. I didn't know her."

Lifting her hand, Barbara stroked his silky mustache. "I know, Thack. What else is in the letter?" she probed gently.

"Oh, that." Thack shrugged. "The letter from the lawyer isn't important." When she frowned he added quickly, "There was a note inside the official letter. A note from my brother." His eyes sparkled like a child's at Christmas. Barbara had to fight the urge to hug him as she would a child.

"What did he write, Thack?" Barbara swallowed against the thickness in her throat.

"Zack wants me to come to California so we can finally meet." Thack hesitated, then rushed on, "Will you come to California with me, Barb?" Again he paused, very briefly. "Come with me as my wife," he finished in a rough, husky tone.

"Oh, Thack, yes!" Barbara cried, hugging him fiercely. Then she remembered the promise she'd made to Dan less than an hour before. "Oh, Thack, I can't!" she groaned, stepping out of his embrace to stare at him despairingly.

"Can't?" Thack grasped her upper arms. "What do you mean you can't?" he demanded.

"I promised Dan—" she began.

"Who is Dan?" Thack's fingers dug relentlessly into her soft flesh.

Barbara smiled into his eyes. "My agent, Mr. Tough Lawman. His name is Dan Greenberg and he's fifty-two years old and very, very married."

"Oh." Thack had the grace to at least *look* disconcerted as he eased his grip on her arms. "Well, what sort of promise did you make to him?"

Her shoulders drooping dejectedly, Barbara related her phone conversation with Dan. As she spoke, Thack's features tautened and his eyes narrowed.

"Call him back," he said tersely when she'd finished. "Tell him you've made other plans."

Though Barbara bristled at the note of command in Thack's tone, she kept her voice free of inflection. "I can't do that, Thack. I owe Dan. He has worked very hard for me for ten years. He has also been a good friend." She lowered her eyes. "Dan was there for me when I needed a friend the most."

"He was there after you left Vanzant?" Thack asked tightly.

"Yes." Barbara squared her shoulders. "But Dan's not the only reason I want to do this job, Thack. I want it for myself as well."

Thack exhaled slowly. "I see." He did that one-arched-brow number on her. "This is the career break you've been waiting for, isn't it?"

Barbara swallowed the angry words that rushed to her lips. Drawing a calming breath, she met his accusing stare directly. "Yes, it could be. But," she went on quickly when his lips twitched sardonically, "that is not the reason I want to do it."

"Sure."

"Dammit, Thack, I love you!" she shouted. "But I need this!" She was so incensed she missed the spasm of surprise that flashed in his eyes. "I need this assignment to prove to myself that I am not a second-rater!" She paused for a breath, then gasped, "Oh!" when he hauled her into his arms.

"You are not a second-rate anything!" Thack's voice was tight with emotion. "Like Ellie's bullion, you are pure gold all the way through." He drew a rasping breath. "You don't have to prove anything—at least not to me." The broad hands that stroked her back had a noticeable tremor. "But, if you feel you must do this, then do it." He gazed down at her from eyes glistening suspiciously. "When—" he cleared his throat "—when are you leaving?"

"This afternoon." Barbara's eyes burned, as did her throat and her chest.

Thack's arms dropped to his side. "And Ellie?" he said harshly. "She should have someone here with her, Barbara."

The burning sensation spread throughout Barbara's entire body. He had not called her honey, or even Barb. "There'll be a woman here by late this afternoon," she replied dully. "J.B. said he'd take care of it for me."

"J.B. would." Turning abruptly, Thack strode to the door. He grasped the knob, then turned back to her. "Maybe this is for the best," he said harshly. "Everything happened too fast between us." He smiled sourly. "I should have known better. My parents' marriage was based on an explosive attraction and it failed. Yeah," he nodded sharply, "maybe we need a little distance between us to put our feelings into perspective."

Too aware of the fact that he had not responded to her shouted avowal of love, Barbara was already feeling the distance, and he was only a few feet away from her. *Oh, damn,* she cried silently, *why did love always have to hurt so very badly?* Afraid to trust her voice, she let a nod suffice for an agreement to his reasoning.

"I'll be at the ranch." Pulling the long envelope from his pocket, he removed the contents then tossed it onto the dresser. "If you want to reach me," he added softly.

Barbara frowned her confusion. "The ranch?" Her gaze sliced to the envelope, then back to him. "How long is your leave for?"

"I'm no longer on leave, Barbara." He twisted the doorknob with controlled violence. "I handed in my resignation this morning." A derisive smile played over his tight lips. "I'll see ya." He pulled the door open, then paused to glance back at her with emotion-darkened eyes. "I love you, you know?" Then he was gone, from the room and the house. Barbara heard the sound of the pickup's engine as he roared from the property.

The entire East Coast lay sweltering and exhausted within the grip of a late summer heat wave. In an elegant Manhattan restaurant, Barbara sat serenely absorbing a blistering lecture from her agent.

"Are you nuts?" Dan hissed with the effort to control his temper. "The Satin Skin people are ecstatic with the commercials you did for them. They want to use you again." He raked a long narrow hand through his thinning hair. "Hell, half a dozen companies want you! How can you sit there and calmly tell me you want to retire?" he demanded.

"Not want, Dan," Barbara corrected him gently. "I *have* retired. That's what I'm calmly telling you."

"But why, Barbara?" Dan gulped at his watered whiskey. "Will you tell me why?"

"I'm in love." Barbara smiled at the grimace that twisted his lips. She knew what he was thinking. After the fiasco of her love affair with Peter, Dan didn't trust her emotional judgment.

"Oh, yeah," he snorted derisively. "The cowboy you told me about."

"Rancher," she again corrected him.

"Whatever!" Dan snarled disparagingly. "Dammit, Babsy! I don't want to see you hurt the way you were the last time." His gaze searched her face, as if looking for signs of pain already. Barbara smiled brilliantly at him. "Besides which, what do you need with a man?" Though she choked on her wine, Dan was oblivious to the incongruity of his question. "You will finally be in a position to grab at the world's tail. How can you throw that away?"

"I don't need or want the world's tail, Dan," she murmured. "All I want is a little section of Texas."

"What the hell's in Texas?" Dan grumbled.

An image of a tall, lean man with white-gold hair and golden bronze skin filled Barbara's mind. A secret smile curved her softened lips as an echo of Thack's description of her rang in her mind.

"Pure gold," she said clearly. "That's what's in Texas for me, Dan."

In the end, Dan gave in, as Barbara had known he would. Standing outside the famous restaurant, he gazed at her sadly, then drew her into his arms to hug her fiercely.

"Keep in touch, Babsy," he instructed in an emotion-thickened voice. "Because, you know, you really are like my own baby."

Barbara unabashedly wiped the tears from her cheeks as she walked away from her best friend. Unmindful of the jostling crowds, or the energy-draining heat, she strode to a small shop on Fifth Avenue.

Inside the shop, Barbara carefully made her selections, then smiled with satisfaction when the package was presented for her inspection before being wrapped for shipping.

The shockingly expensive chocolates looked mouth-wateringly delicious nestled inside the gold-toned box. At her nod of approval, the box was tied with a gold string. Barbara had penned a brief message on the gift card that was to accompany the box. Ten words were all she required to say what was in her heart. The card read: *What's the weather like in California this time of year?*

As she paid for the chocolates, Barbara was struck by the realization that with the gold-toned box, she was literally gambling with her future. More apprehensive than she cared to admit, she left the shop and went back to her apartment to await the results of her actions.

Three weeks had elapsed since she'd returned to the city. Three weeks in which she'd received no word by phone or letter from Thack. Barbara knew from her aunt Ellie's letters that Thack had returned to his ranch near San Antonio. And that was the extent of what she knew.

How would Thack react to the chocolates and the note it contained? The question was Barbara's constant companion as she prowled the three rooms of her apartment. The lack of communication from him had been hard to bear while she'd been busy doing the commercials for the Satin Skin company. With no assignments to rush to, no classes to attend, the time dragged at her confidence and her nerves.

How long did it take for a package to go from New York to Texas? Barbara continually upbraided herself for not enquiring about the time element involved in the shipping.

And now, finally at liberty to eat whatever she wished, she hungered for nothing—except the sight of a tall, laid-back Texan.

By the evening of the fourth day, Barbara was on the verge of tearing her hair. The only thing that kept her from breaking down was the memory of his parting words to her: *I love you, you know.*

At sundown, she began repeating the words to herself; by 9:15 P.M. she was speaking the words aloud like a litany. Her cadence was broken by the buzz of the building intercom. Startled, she walked over to the unit mounted on the wall.

"Yes?" she responded distractedly.

"Ms. Holcomb," the security doorman said respectfully. "There's a long, tall Texan in the lobby by name of Sharp who insists you want to see him." Amusement lurked in his solemn tone. "Should I let him come up?"

"Yes." The assent shuddered from Barbara's trembling lips. "Oh, yes, please!"

Thack. As she replaced the unit's receiver Barbara closed her eyes. *Thack.* She forced herself to breathe deeply several times to combat a sudden sensation of lightheadedness. Then, her eyes flying open, she ran for the door, cursing the wasted minutes required to flip the three security locks. Finally flinging the door wide open she dashed into the hall just as the ping sounded from the elevator and the doors swished apart. Two women stepped from the car, and close on their heels was a tall man in a tan, Western-style suit, tan boots, and a spotless cream-colored Stetson. Barbara's breath caught in her throat, then, with a strangled cry, she was running along the hallway.

"Thack!"

Tears streaming down her cheeks, Barbara launched herself into Thack's outstretched arms. Encircling his waist she held on for dear life, sighing with a sensation of homecoming when he crushed her to his hard length.

"I was so afraid!" She sobbed into his silky brown shirt. "Oh, Thack, I was really getting scared." Tilting her head back, she glared up at him. "What took you so long—dammit!"

Barbara could hear the sound of muffled giggles coming from the two women who were unabashedly watching them. Enchanted by the beautiful smile on Thack's handsome face, Barbara ignored them.

"Your message arrived late this afternoon," Thack murmured as he lowered his head to hers. "I was off the property and in the air within the hour." His last word was lost as his lips touched Barbara's mouth.

Every one of Barbara's senses rejoiced at the gliding motion of his lips molding to hers, his tongue seeking her sweetness. She didn't even hear the gentle sighs from the women watching behind them. But Thack did.

Without breaking the kiss, he swept her off her feet and high into his arms. Carrying her effortlessly, he strode to the open doorway. Then, raising his head, he turned back to face the wide-eyed women. Jostling Barbara, he managed to bring up his hand to tip the Stetson at the flushed females.

"Evenin' ladies," he drawled. Slanting a wicked grin at Barbara, he strode into the apartment and closed the door with a backward kick of one booted foot. As the door slammed, shutting them in together, Thack arched his brow at her and said one distinct word.

"Where?"

Happiness and excitement rushing to her head, Barbara indicated her bedroom with a flick of her hand.

The bedroom door was closed with another booted kick. As he set her on her feet beside the bed, Thack issued a teasingly growled warning.

"If you swear one more time, *I* swear I'll take up smoking again."

Laughing, crying, loving him till it hurt, Barbara reached up to grasp his head with her trembling hands. "You big goof!" she sniffled. "Do you know I haven't had a cigarette since I got back!"

Thack's smile brought goose bumps to the surface of her skin. "Lost the craving, huh?" His smile turned so sexy she felt a flash of heat to the soles of her feet. "Or, maybe it's been replaced by a different kind of craving...um?"

"Chocolate, you mean?" Barbara stared at him from innocent wide eyes.

"I told you, honey." Thack's fingers were working deftly as they gathered the folds of her caftan, inexorably drawing it up her body. "Chocolate is *second* best."

The caftan sailed through the air before floating onto the floor. Standing before him in nothing but very brief panties, Barbara shivered in response to the warm, hungry look in his eyes.

"God, I missed you," Thack muttered hoarsely, his long fingers unfastening the buttons on his shirt.

"Has there been enough time and distance?" Barbara asked raggedly as shirt and suit jacket joined her caftan.

"Too much time." One boot thumped to the floor. "And much too much distance." The second boot made a like noise. "I'm about to close the distance." Suit pants and cotton briefs slid down his legs. "And make up for lost time." Picking her up, he placed her on the bed. "Right now." As he dropped to the bed beside her, his mouth unerringly found hers.

There was no time or desire for preliminary caressing. But, as he poised over her, Thack stared deeply into Barbara's passion-bright eyes. Once again his voice held that heart-wrenchingly uncertain edge.

"Do you still love me, Barb?"

"Yes," she whispered from a throat tight with emotion.

Thack swallowed with obvious difficulty. "Then, could you kind'a shout it at me like you did before?"

"I love you, Thackery Sharp!" Barbara shouted joyfully.

"Now you're talkin'."

Barbara had a glimpse of his flashing smile, then his mouth took hers, hungrily, urgently. The time for words was past. Responding to emotional needs intensified by three weeks' worth of uncertainty and longing, she grasped his hair with trembling fingers, tugging him to her with a silent, yet eloquent, demand.

Thack answered her demand with the bold thrust of his tongue, initiating a rhythm evocative of the deeper, more intimate invasion to follow. Like molten fire, Barbara's body swirled around him, her quivering thighs and arching hips an erotic invitation.

Groaning, Thack released her mouth to glide his lips down her arched throat. "Barb, honey, I'm sorry," he muttered against her heated skin. "I wanted to make it perfect for you...but, these last weeks have stretched my control about as far as it will go." He clasped her hips with hands every bit as unsteady as her own, lifting her as he lowered his body. "I need you so much, honey," he whispered harshly. "I need you so very much."

"And I need you," Barbara moaned, then gasped as an electric shock of pleasure pierced her when his body thrust into hers. And then the only sounds to break the quiet in the room were the breathless, inarticulate murmurings of giving and taking in kind.

His long body taut with strain, Thack drove himself relentlessly toward the pinnacle of physical pleasure, shuddering with the realization that Barbara was with him every sensuous moment of the way.

Going over the crest was not unlike being flung into a vortex of shimmering ecstasy, doubly intensified by their simultaneous explosion.

Shaken by the sudden, exquisite release from inner turbulence, Barbara clung to Thack's sweat-dampened back, unaware that her nails were inflicting crescents in his smooth skin, or that the quivering exultant tremor in her voice enriched his deep satisfaction.

"Thackery! Thackery!" She wanted to say more, tell him of the euphoric completion he had given her. But all that came out was the prayerlike whisper of his name.

Thack heard every unspoken thought contained within Barbara's husky tone. Quaking inside from the awesome experience, he held her tightly, possessively, protectively. Unformed, yet certain, a vow was cast in steel in his mind; never again would he let this woman out of his sight. She was his, as irrevocably as he was hers.

Easing onto the bed beside her, Thack drew Barbara into his arms, and very safe keeping.

The phone woke Barbara at seven-forty the following morning. Aching from the glorious activity Thack had engaged her in throughout most of the night, she groaned and reached for the shrilling instrument.

"Hello?" she muttered without opening her eyes.

"Good morning, Barbara, I'm sorry if I woke you."

Barbara's eyes flew wide at the sound of Peter Vanzant's deep voice. "It—it's all right." She blinked, "Ah . . . what . . . is something wrong, Peter?" With the mention of the name she felt Thack stiffen beside her.

"What does he want?" Thack's voice was low, and dangerous. Even as she was lifting her shoulders helplessly, Peter let her know he'd heard the snarled question.

"There's someone with you," Peter remarked. "Would it be more convenient if I called you back?"

"No, Peter." Barbara gazed lovingly into Thack's glittering eyes. "I won't be here later. I'm going to California on my honeymoon, then to my husband's ranch in Texas." A smile curved her lips as she watched the tension ease out of Thack's body. "Why did you call, Peter?"

"It's Nicole," he said. "She has finally decided to rejoin the world. I was going to ask you to take her under your wing, keep an eye on her." He sighed, surprising Barbara. Peter never sighed! "I'm sorry I bothered you, Barbara. I hope you'll be happy on that ranch in Texas," he said deeply. "And I mean that sincerely."

"Thank you, Peter." Barbara smiled brilliantly at Thack. "I know I'll be happy. I love him very much." She muffled a yelp as Thack hauled her against him. She was about to respond to Peter's farewell when a thought struck. "Peter! Tell Nicole that if she's ever in Texas, and needs a friend, she is always welcome." She raised her brows questioningly at Thack. Nodding agreement, he murmured the address she had committed to memory. After repeating the address to Peter, she gently replaced the receiver.

"Had me going there for a minute," Thack muttered, drawing her down beside him. "I thought I was going to have to challenge him to a shoot-out in the middle of Times Square."

"Do you love me that much, Thack?" she asked, not altogether teasingly.

"Yes." Thack didn't hesitate.

"Then, could you kind'a shout it at me?"

"I love you, Barbara Holcomb...Honey!"

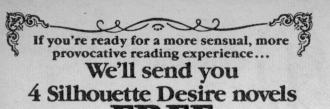

ⅅ Silhouette Desire

COMING NEXT MONTH

TREASURE HUNT—Maura Seger
When Lucas and Emily dove for sunken diamonds, the modern-day pirates after them weren't the only danger. They recovered the treasure, but they lost their hearts—to each other.

THE MYTH AND THE MAGIC—Christine Flynn
Combining Stephanie's impulsiveness and Adam's scientific logic meant nothing but trouble. Mythical beast or archaeological abnormality—could the fossil they found lead to the magic of love?

LOVE UNDERCOVER—Sandra Kleinschmit
After reporter Brittany Daniels and detective Gabe Spencer got used to the idea that they needed one another to crack a case, they soon discovered that work and play needn't be mutally exclusive.

DESTINY'S DAUGHTER—Elaine Camp
Years before, Banner's mother had deserted her family for the love of another man. Yuri was that man's son. Could they let the past they couldn't control destroy their chance for a future?

MOMENT OF TRUTH—Suzanne Simms
Michael just couldn't get Alexa out of his mind. Her flamboyance wreaked havoc with his stuffy pin-striped orthodoxy, but when they kissed they had to face the facts: this was love.

SERENDIPITY SAMANTHA—Jo Ann Algermissen
She was an inventor, and nothing could distract her from her work until she met Jack Martin, and a flash of genius became a flash of desire.

AVAILABLE NOW: